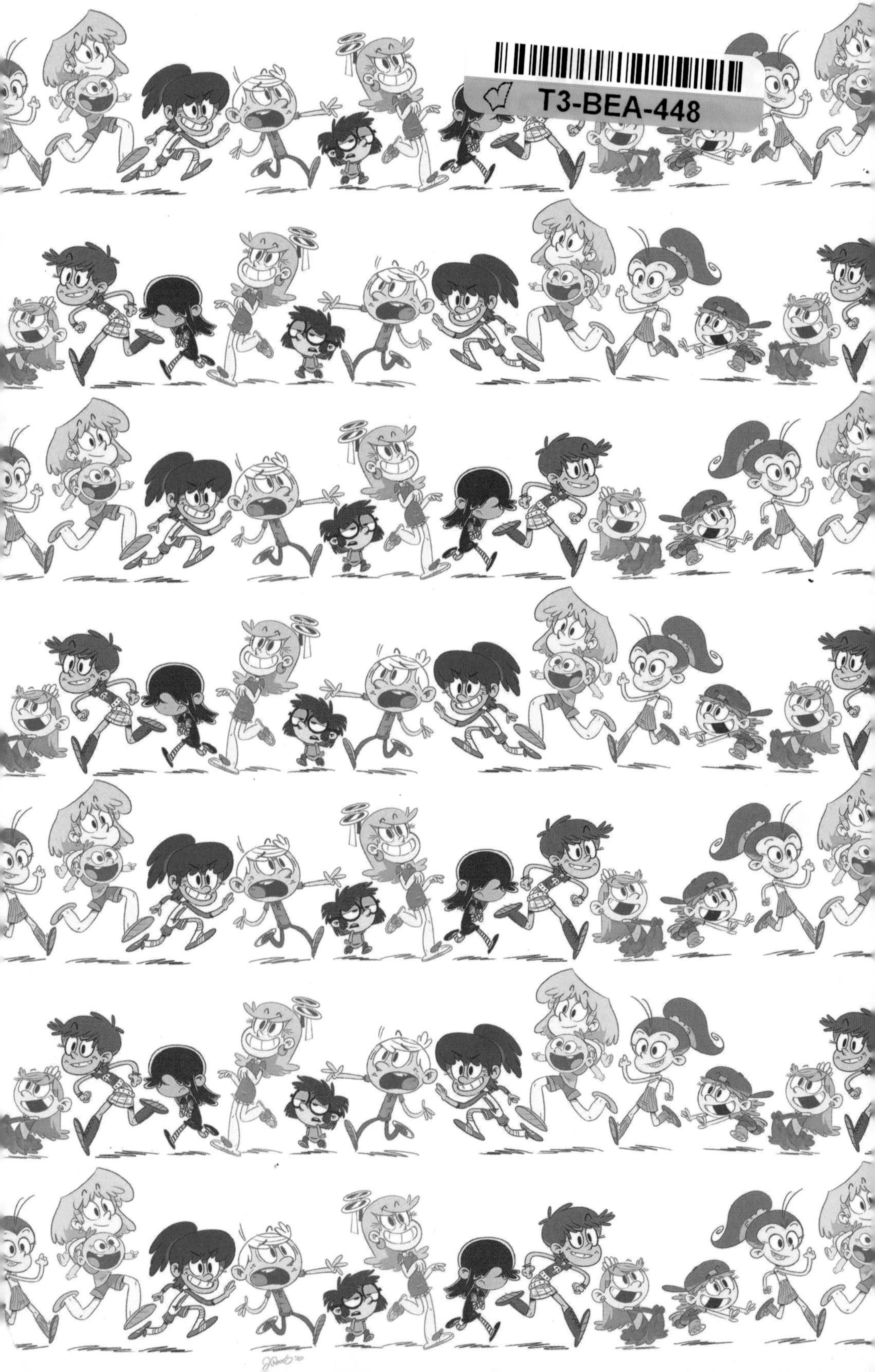

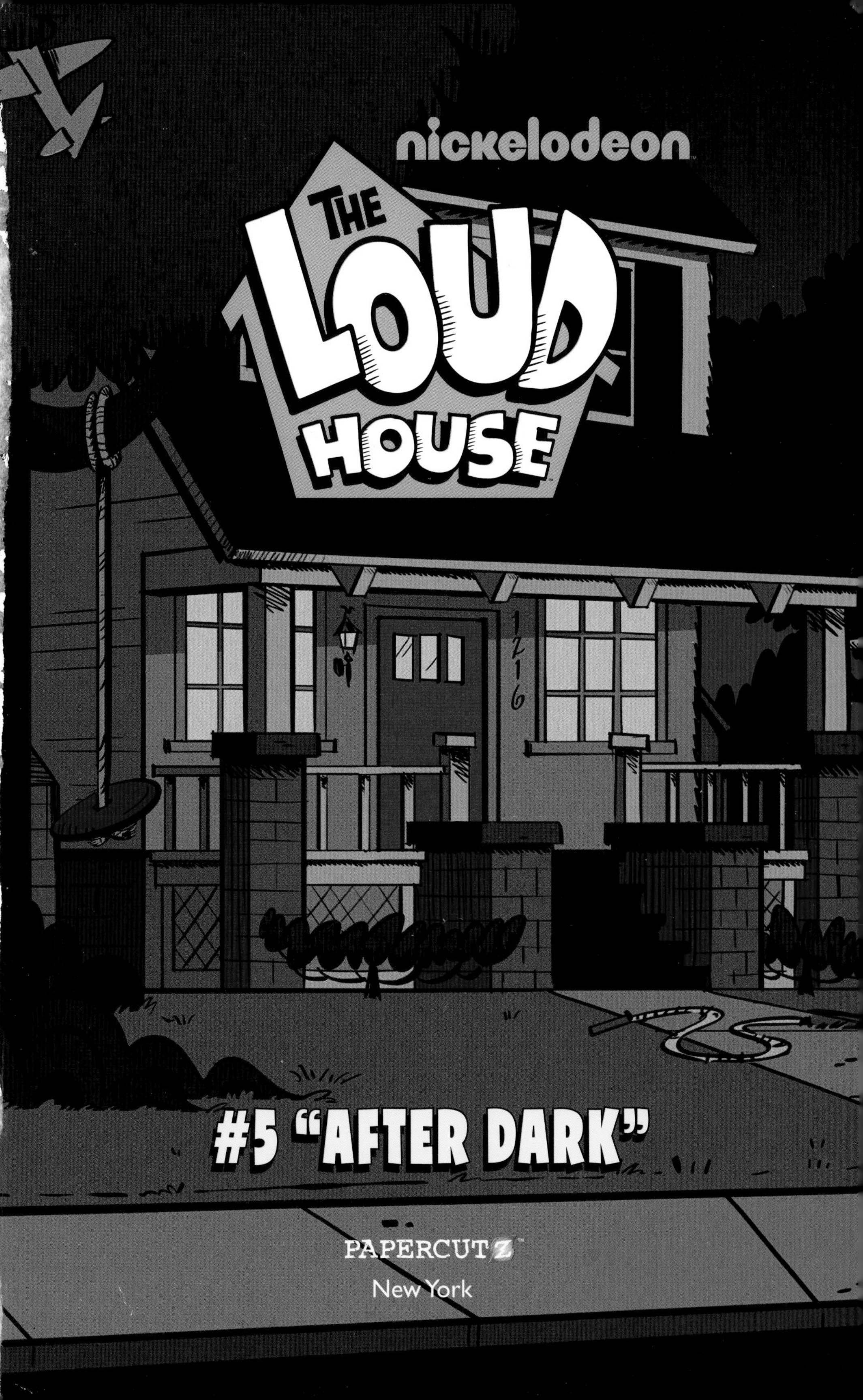

nickelodeon

THE LOUD HOUSE

#5 "AFTER DARK"

PAPERCUTZ
New York

nickelodeon GRAPHIC NOVELS AVAILABLE FROM PAPERCUTZ

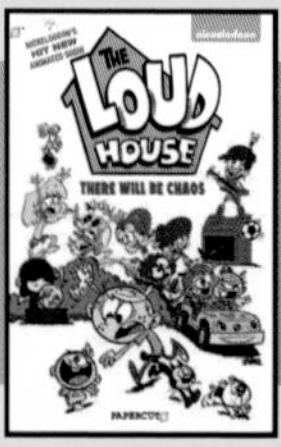
THE LOUD HOUSE
THERE WILL BE CHAOS
THE LOUD HOUSE #1 "There Will Be Chaos"

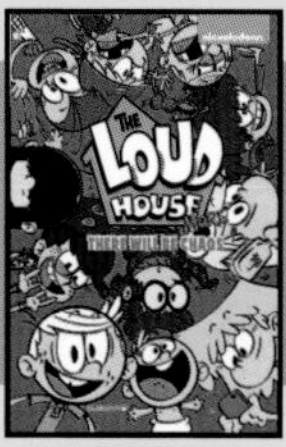
THE LOUD HOUSE
THE LOUD HOUSE #2 "There Will Be More Chaos"

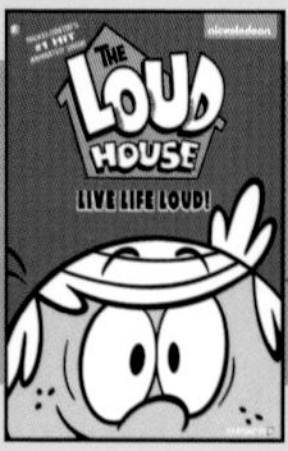
THE LOUD HOUSE
LIVE LIFE LOUD!
THE LOUD HOUSE #3 "Live Life Loud!"

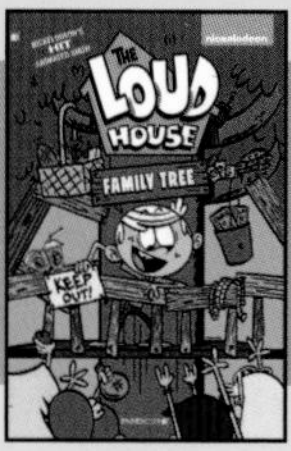
THE LOUD HOUSE
FAMILY TREE
THE LOUD HOUSE #4 "Family Tree"

COMING SOON!

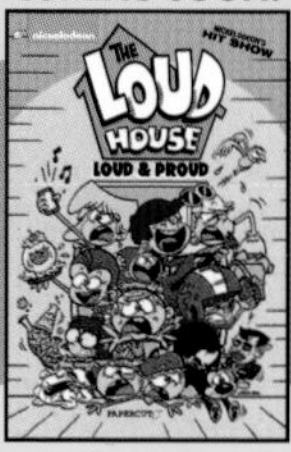
THE LOUD HOUSE
LOUD & PROUD
THE LOUD HOUSE #6 "Loud and Proud"

Collecting Loud House 1-3

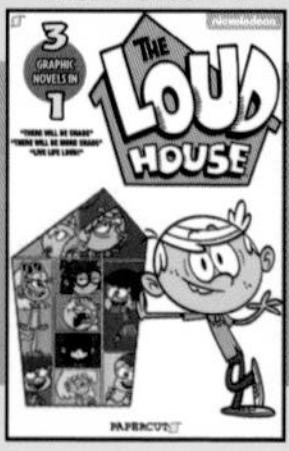
THE LOUD HOUSE
THE LOUD HOUSE 3 IN 1 #1

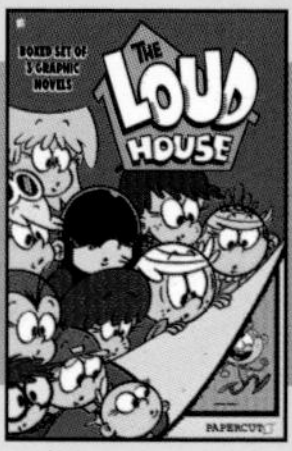
THE LOUD HOUSE
THE LOUD HOUSE BOXED SET $23.99

THESE ALSO INCLUDE LOUD HOUSE STORIES!

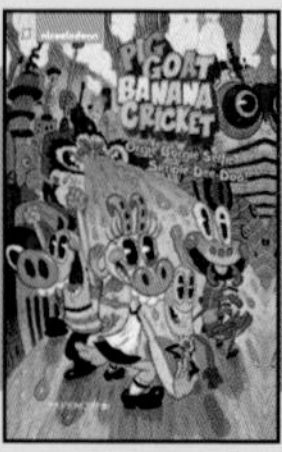
PIG GOAT BANANA CRICKET
PIG GOAT BANANA CRICKET #1 "Orgle Borgle Selfie Simple-Dee Doo!"

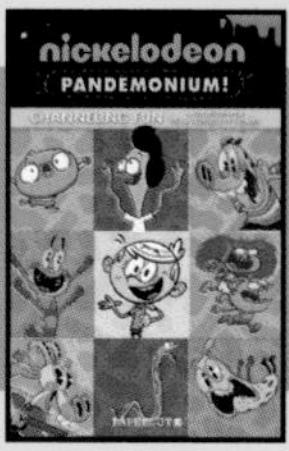
nickelodeon
PANDEMONIUM!
NICKELODEON PANDEMONIUM #1 "Channeling Fun"

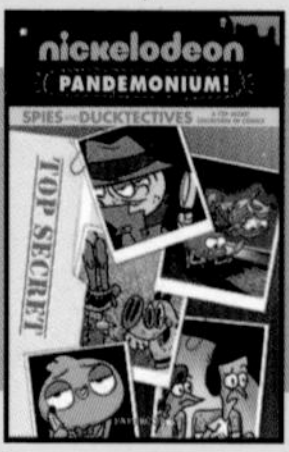
nickelodeon
PANDEMONIUM!
SPIES AND DUCKTECTIVES
TOP SECRET
NICKELODEON PANDEMONIUM #2 "Spies and Ducktectives"

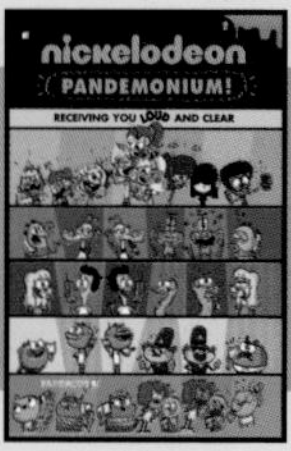
nickelodeon
PANDEMONIUM!
NICKELODEON PANDEMONIUM #3 "Receiving You Loud and Clear"

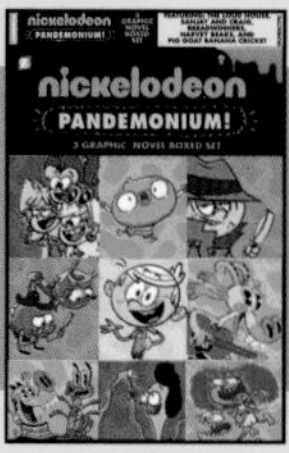
nickelodeon
PANDEMONIUM!
NICKELODEON PANDEMONIUM BOXED SET $24.99

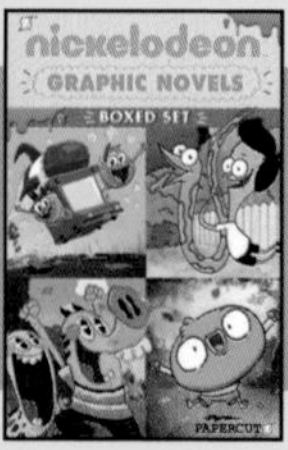
nickelodeon
GRAPHIC NOVELS
BOXED SET
NICKELODEON BOXED SET $31.99

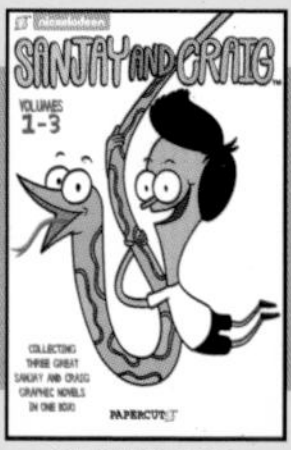
SANJAY AND CRAIG
VOLUMES 1-3
SANJAY AND CRAIG BOXED SET $23.99

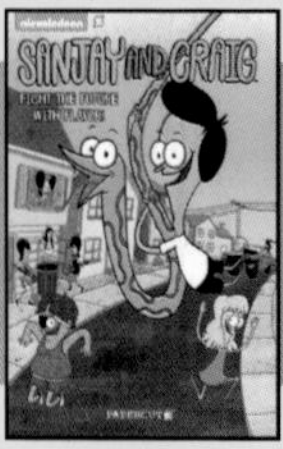
SANJAY AND CRAIG
SANJAY AND CRAIG #1 "Fight the Future with Flavor"

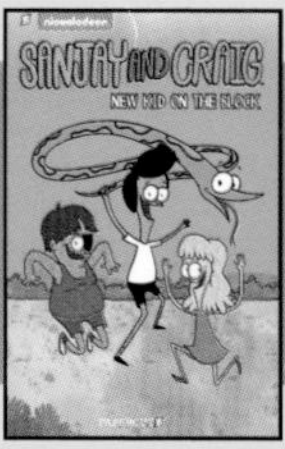
SANJAY AND CRAIG
NEW KID ON THE BLOCK
SANJAY AND CRAIG #2 "New Kid on the Block"

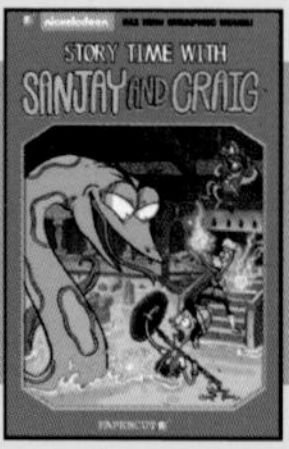
STORY TIME WITH
SANJAY AND CRAIG
SANJAY AND CRAIG #3 "Story Time with Sanjay and Craig"

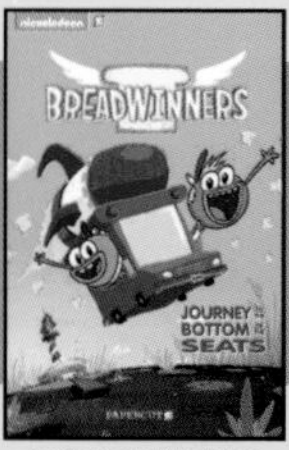
BREADWINNERS
JOURNEY TO THE BOTTOM OF THE SEATS
BREADWINNERS #1 "Journey to the Bottom of the Seats"

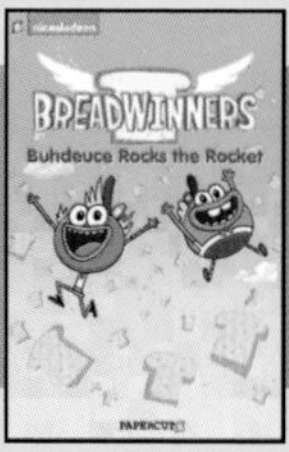
BREADWINNERS
Buhdeuce Rocks the Rocket
BREADWINNERS #2 "Buhdeuce Rocks the Rocket"

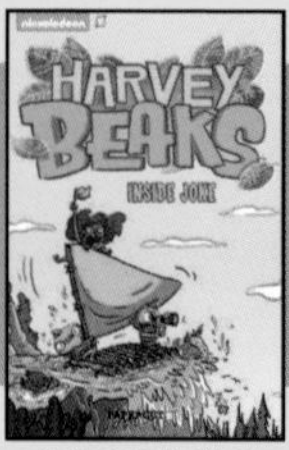
HARVEY BEAKS
INSIDE JOKE
HARVEY BEAKS #1 "Inside Joke"

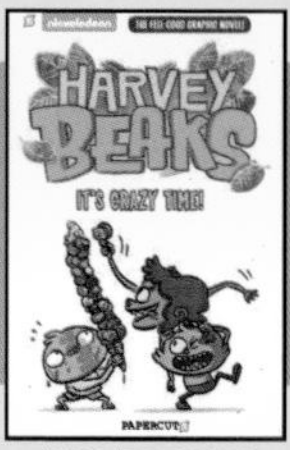
HARVEY BEAKS
IT'S CRAZY TIME!
HARVEY BEAKS #2 "It's Crazy Time"

Nickelodeon graphic novels are available for $7.99 each in paperback, $12.99 each in hardcover. NICKELODEON PANDEMONIUM #3 is $8.99 each in paperback, $13.99 each in hardcover. BOXED SETS differ in price. Available from booksellers everywhere. You can also order online from Papercutz.com, or call 1-800-886-1223, Monday through Friday, 9-5 EST. MC, Visa, and AmEx accepted. To order by mail, please add $5.00 for postage and handling for the first book ordered, $1.00 for each additional book and make check payable to NBM Publishing. Send to: Papercutz, 160 Broadway, Suite 700, East Wing, New York, NY 10038.

Nickelodeon graphic novels are also available digitally wherever e-books are sold.

THE LOUD HOUSE

#5 "AFTER DARK"

nickelodeon THE LOUD HOUSE #5 "AFTER DARK"

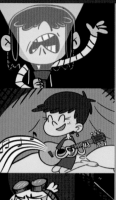

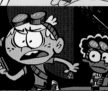

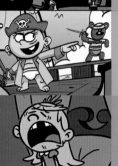

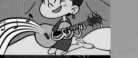

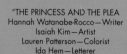

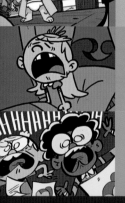

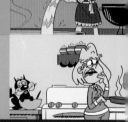

"GHOST OF THE TOWN"
Sammie Crowley—Writer
Ari Castleton—Artist
Gabrielle Dolbey—Colorist
Ida Hem—Letterer

"DRAWING A PRANK"
Andrew Brooks—Writer
David Teas—Artist, Colorist
Ida Hem—Letterer

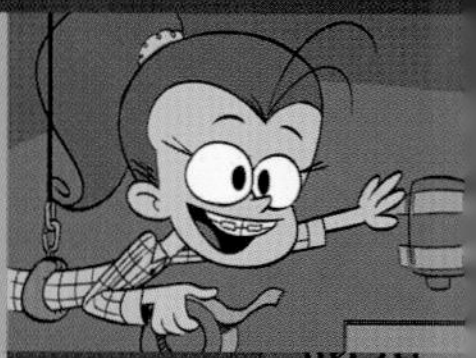

"MIDNIGHT MELODY"
Hannah Watanabe-Rocco—
Writer, Artist, Colorist
Ida Hem—Letterer

"GOAL-ORIENTED"
Andrew Brooks—Writer
Gabrielle Dolbey—Artist, Colorist
Ida Hem—Letterer

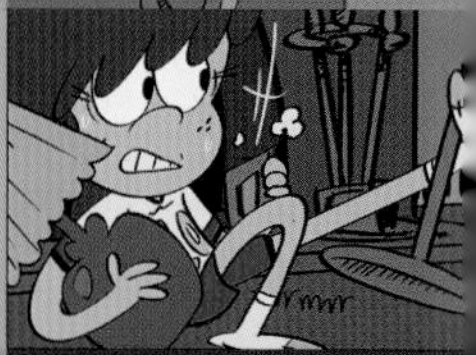

"GHOST IN THE BASEMENT"
Sammie Crowley—Writer
Ari Castleton—Artist
Gabrielle Dolbey—Colorist
Ida Hem—Letterer

"THE EARLY BIRDS AND THE WORMS"
Kevin Sullivan—Writer
Ida Hem—Artist, Letterer
Hallie Wilson—Colorist

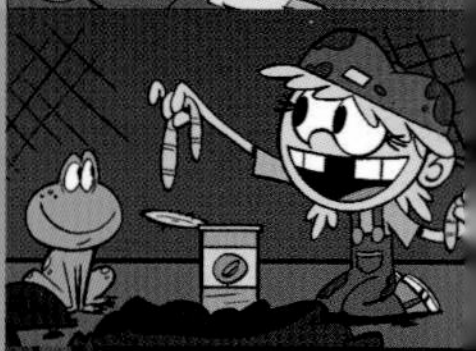

"SHIPS IN THE NIGHT"
Sammie Crowley—Writer
Gizelle Orbino (Lisa's room), Marcus
Velazquez (Dream sequence)—Artists,
Colorists
Ida Hem—Letterer

"BUSTED!"
Sammie Crowley—Writer
Ari Castleton—Artist
Gabrielle Dolbey—Colorist
Ida Hem—Letterer

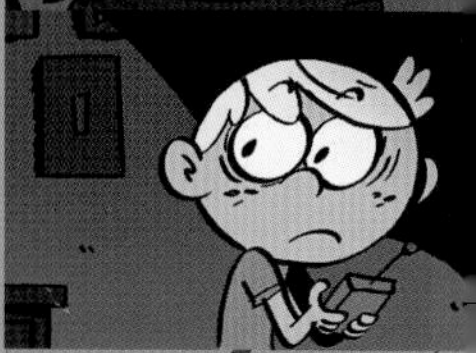

"THE PRINCESS AND THE PLEA
Hannah Watanabe-Rocco—Writer
Isaiah Kim—Artist
Lauren Patterson—Colorist
Ida Hem—Letterer

"TUB TIME"
Kevin Sullivan—Writer
Ashley Kliment—Artist, Letterer
Colton Davis—Colorist
Ida Hem—Letterer

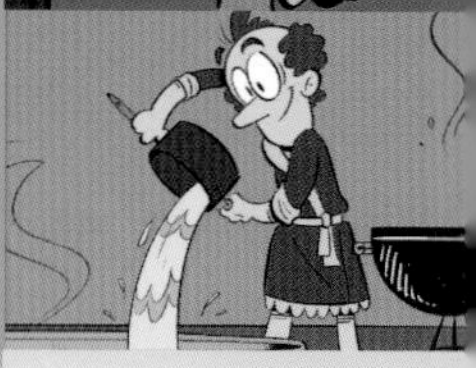

"BOYS IN THE ATTIC"
Sammie Crowley—Writer
Ari Castleton—Artist
Gabrielle Dolbey—Colorist
Ida Hem—Letterer

"BREAKFAST IS READY!"
Kevin Sullivan—Writer
Angela Entzminger—Artist, Colorist
Ida Hem—Letterer

JARED MORGAN—Cover Artist
JORDAN ROSATO—Endpapers
JAMES SALERNO—Sr. Art Director/Nickelodeon
JAYJAY JACKSON—Design
SEAN GANTKA, ANGELA ENTZMINGER, SAMMIE CROWLEY, DANA CLUVERIUS, MOLLIE FREILICH,
AMANDA RYNDA, MIGUEL PUGA, DIEM DOAN, DAWN GUZZO—Special Thanks
JEFF WHITMAN—Editor
JOAN HILTY—Comics Editor/Nickelodeon
JIM SALICRUP
Editor-in-Chief

ISBN: 978-1-5458-0154-3 paperback edition
ISBN: 978-1-5458-0153-6 hardcover edition

Printed in India
November 2018

Distributed by Macmillan
First Printing

MEET THE LOUD FAMILY *and friends!*

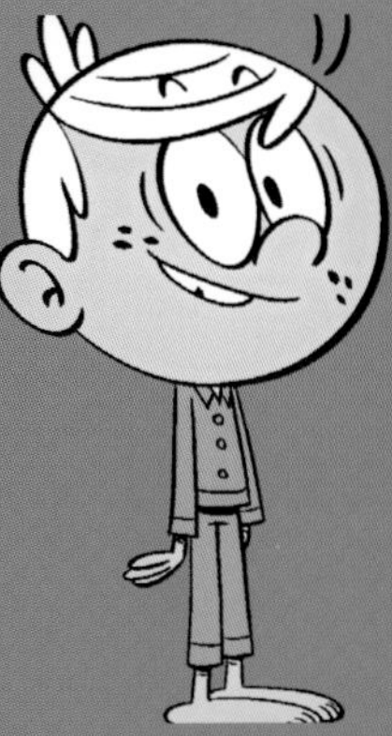

LINCOLN LOUD
THE MIDDLE CHILD (11)

At 11 years old, Lincoln is the middle child, with five older sisters and five younger sisters. He has learned that surviving the Loud household means staying a step ahead. He's the man with a plan, always coming up with a way to get what he wants or deal with a problem, even if things inevitably go wrong. Being the only boy comes with some perks. Lincoln gets his own room – even if it's just a converted linen closet. On the other hand, being the only boy also means he sometimes gets a little too much attention from his sisters. They mother him, tease him, and use him as the occasional lab rat or fashion show participant. Lincoln's sisters may drive him crazy, but he loves them and is always willing to help out if they need him.

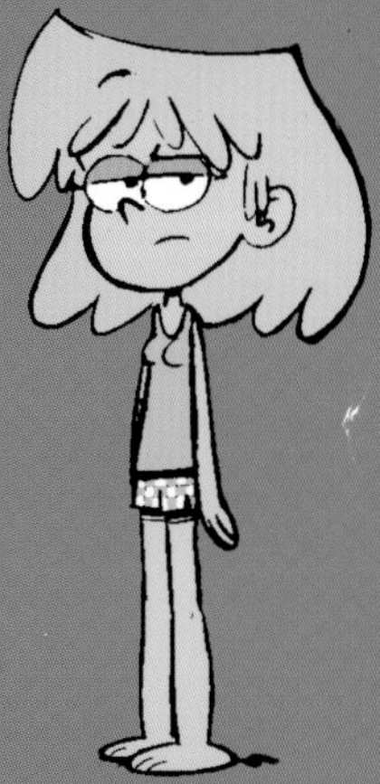

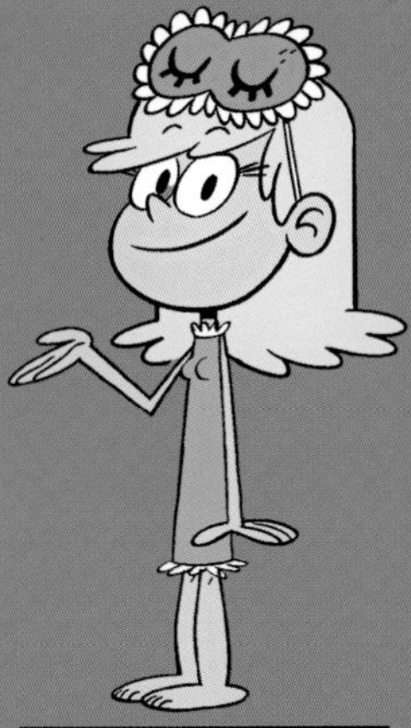

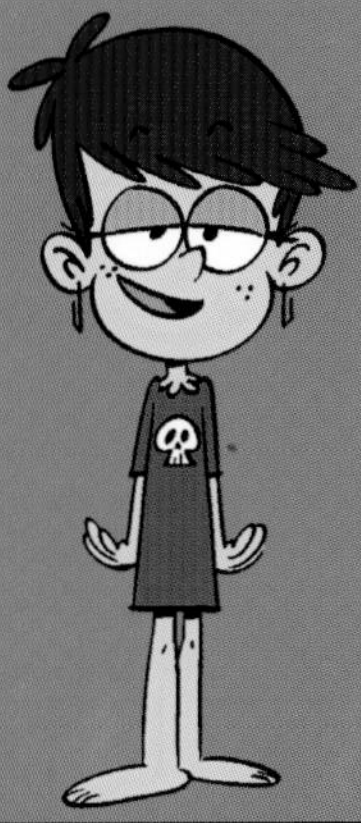

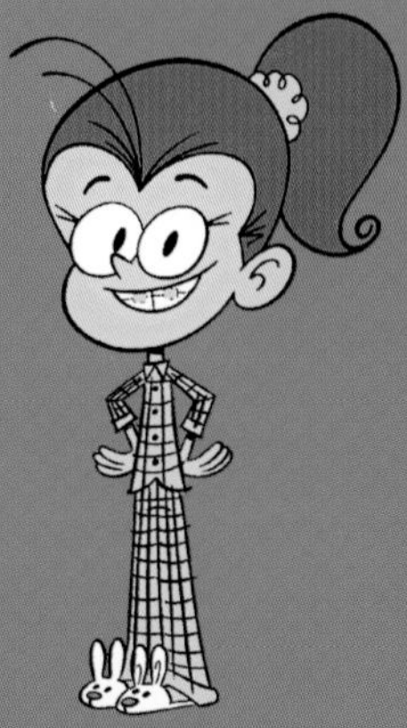

LORI LOUD
THE OLDEST (17)

As the first-born child of the Loud clan, Lori sees herself as the boss of all her siblings. She feels she's paved the way for them and deserves extra respect. Her signature traits are rolling her eyes, texting her boyfriend Bobby, and literally saying "literally" all the time. Because she's the oldest and most experienced sibling, Lori can be a great ally, so it pays to stay on her good side.

LENI LOUD
THE FASHIONISTA (16)

Leni spends most of her time designing outfits and accessorizing. She always falls for Luan's pranks, and sometimes walks into walls when she's talking (she's not great at doing two things at once). Leni might be flighty, but she's the sweetest of the Loud siblings and truly has a heart of gold (even though she's pretty sure it's a heart of blood).

LUNA LOUD
THE ROCK STAR (15)

Luna is loud, boisterous and freewheeling, and her energy is always cranked to 11. She thinks about music so much that she even talks in song lyrics. On the off-chance she doesn't have her guitar with her, everything can and will be turned into a musical instrument. You can always count on Luna to help out, and she'll do most anything you ask, as long as you're okay with her supplying a rocking guitar accompaniment.

LUAN LOUD
THE JOKESTER (14)

Luan's a standup comedienne who provides a nonstop barrage of silly puns. She's big on prop comedy too – squirting flowers and whoopee cushions – so you have to be on your toes whenever she's around. She loves to pull pranks and is a really good ventriloquist – she is often found doing bits with her dummy, Mr. Coconuts. Luan never lets anything get her down; to her, laughter IS the best medicine.

LYNN LOUD
THE ATHLETE (13)

Lynn is athletic and full of energy and is always looking for a teammate. With her, it's all sports all the time. She'll turn anything into a sport. Putting away eggs? Jump shot! Score! Cleaning up the eggs? Slap shot! Score! Lynn is very competitive, tends to be superstitious about her teams, and accepts almost any dare.

LUCY LOUD
THE EMO (8)

You can always count on Lucy to give the morbid point of view in any given situation. She is obsessed with all things spooky and dark – funerals, vampires, séances, and the like. She wears mostly black and writes moody poetry. She's usually quiet and keeps to herself. Lucy has a way of mysteriously appearing out of nowhere, and try as they might, her siblings never get used to this.

LOLA LOUD
THE BEAUTY QUEEN (6)

Lola could not be more different from her twin sister, Lana. She's a pageant powerhouse whose interests include glitter, photo shoots, and her own beautiful, beautiful face. But don't let her cute, gap-toothed smile fool you; underneath all the sugar and spice lurks a Machiavellian mastermind. Whatever Lola wants, Lola gets – or else. She's the eyes and ears of the household and never resists an opportunity to tattle on troublemakers. But if you stay on Lola's good side, you've got yourself a fierce ally – and a lifetime supply of free makeovers.

LANA LOUD
THE TOMBOY (6)

Lana is the rough-and-tumble sparkplug counterpart to her twin sister, Lola. She's all about reptiles, mud pies, and muffler repair. She's the resident Ms. Fix-it and is always ready to lend a hand – the dirtier the job, the better. Need your toilet unclogged? Snake fed? Back-zit popped? Lana's your gal. All she asks in return is a little A-B-C gum, or a handful of kibble (she often sneaks it from the dog bowl).

LISA LOUD
THE GENIUS (4)

Lisa is smarter than the rest of her siblings combined. She'll most likely be a rocket scientist, or a brain surgeon, or an evil genius who takes over the world. Lisa spends most of her time working in her lab (the family has gotten used to the explosions), and says her research leaves little time for frivolous human pursuits like "playing" or "getting haircuts." That said, she's always there to help with a homework question, or to explain why the sky is blue, or to point out the structural flaws in someone's pillow fort. Lisa says it's the least she can do for her favorite test subjects, er, siblings.

LILY LOUD
THE BABY (15 MONTHS)

Lily is a giggly, drooly, diaper-ditching free spirit, affectionately known as "the poop machine." You can't keep a nappy on this kid – she's like a teething Houdini. But even when Lily's running wild, dropping rancid diaper bombs, or drooling all over the remote, she always brings a smile to everyone's face (and a clothespin to their nose). Lily is everyone's favorite little buddy, and the whole family loves her unconditionally.

RITA LOUD

Mother to the eleven Loud kids, Mom (Rita Loud) wears many different hats. She's a chauffeur, homework-checker and barf-cleaner-upper all rolled into one. She's always there for her kids and ready to jump into action during a crisis, whether it's a fight between the twins or Leni's missing shoe. When she's not chasing the kids around or at her day job as a dental hygienist, Mom pursues her passion: writing. She also loves taking on house projects and is very handy with tools (guess that's where Lana gets it from). Between writing, working, and being a mom, her days are always hectic but she wouldn't have it any other way.

LYNN LOUD SR.

Dad (Lynn Loud Sr.) is a fun-loving, upbeat aspiring chef. A kid-at-heart, he's not above taking part in the kids' zany schemes. In addition to cooking, Dad loves his van, playing the cowbell, and making puns. Before meeting Mom, Dad spent a semester in England and has been obsessed with British culture ever since – and sometimes "accidentally" slips into a British accent. When Dad's not wrangling the kids, he's pursuing his dream of opening his own restaurant where he hopes to make his "Lynn-sagnas" world-famous.

FANGS

WALT

BITEY

HOPS

GEO

CLIFF

CHARLES

CLYDE McBRIDE
THE BEST FRIEND (11)

Clyde is Lincoln's partner in crime. He's always willing to go along with Lincoln's crazy schemes (even if he sees the flaws in them up front). Lincoln and Clyde are two peas in a pod and share pretty much all of the same tastes in movies, comics, TV shows, toys – you name it. As an only child, Clyde envies Lincoln – how cool would it be to always have siblings around to talk to? But since Clyde spends so much time at the Loud household, he's almost an honorary sibling anyway. He also has a major crush on Lori.

SAM SHARP

Sam, 15, is Luna's classmate and good friend, who Luna has a crush on. Sam is all about the music – she loves to play guitar and write and compose music. Her favorite genre is rock and roll but she appreciates all good tunes. Unlike Luna, Sam only has one sibling, Simon, but she thinks even one provides enough chaos for her.

MR. BUD GROUSE

Mr. Grouse is the Louds's next-door-neighbor. The Louds often go to him for favors which he normally rejects – unless there's a chance for him to score one of Dad's famous Lynn-sagnas. Mr. Grouse loves gardening, relaxing in his recliner, and keeping anything of the Louds's that flies into his yard (his catchphrase, after all, is "my yard, my property!").

"10:55 PM: GHOST OF THE TOWN"

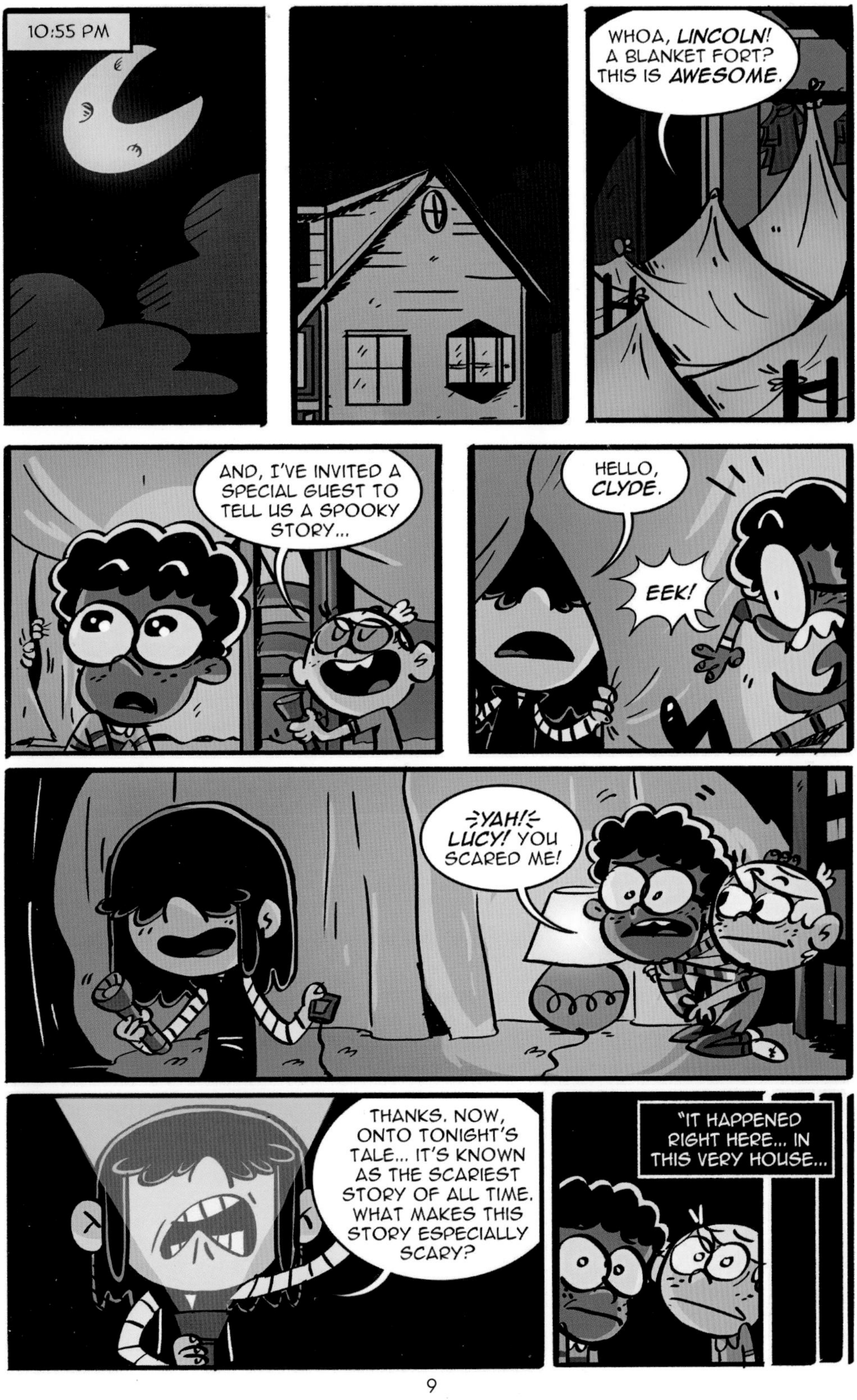
10:55 PM
WHOA, LINCOLN! A BLANKET FORT? THIS IS AWESOME.
AND, I'VE INVITED A SPECIAL GUEST TO TELL US A SPOOKY STORY...
HELLO, CLYDE.
EEK!
YAH! LUCY! YOU SCARED ME!
THANKS. NOW, ONTO TONIGHT'S TALE... IT'S KNOWN AS THE SCARIEST STORY OF ALL TIME. WHAT MAKES THIS STORY ESPECIALLY SCARY?
"IT HAPPENED RIGHT HERE... IN THIS VERY HOUSE...

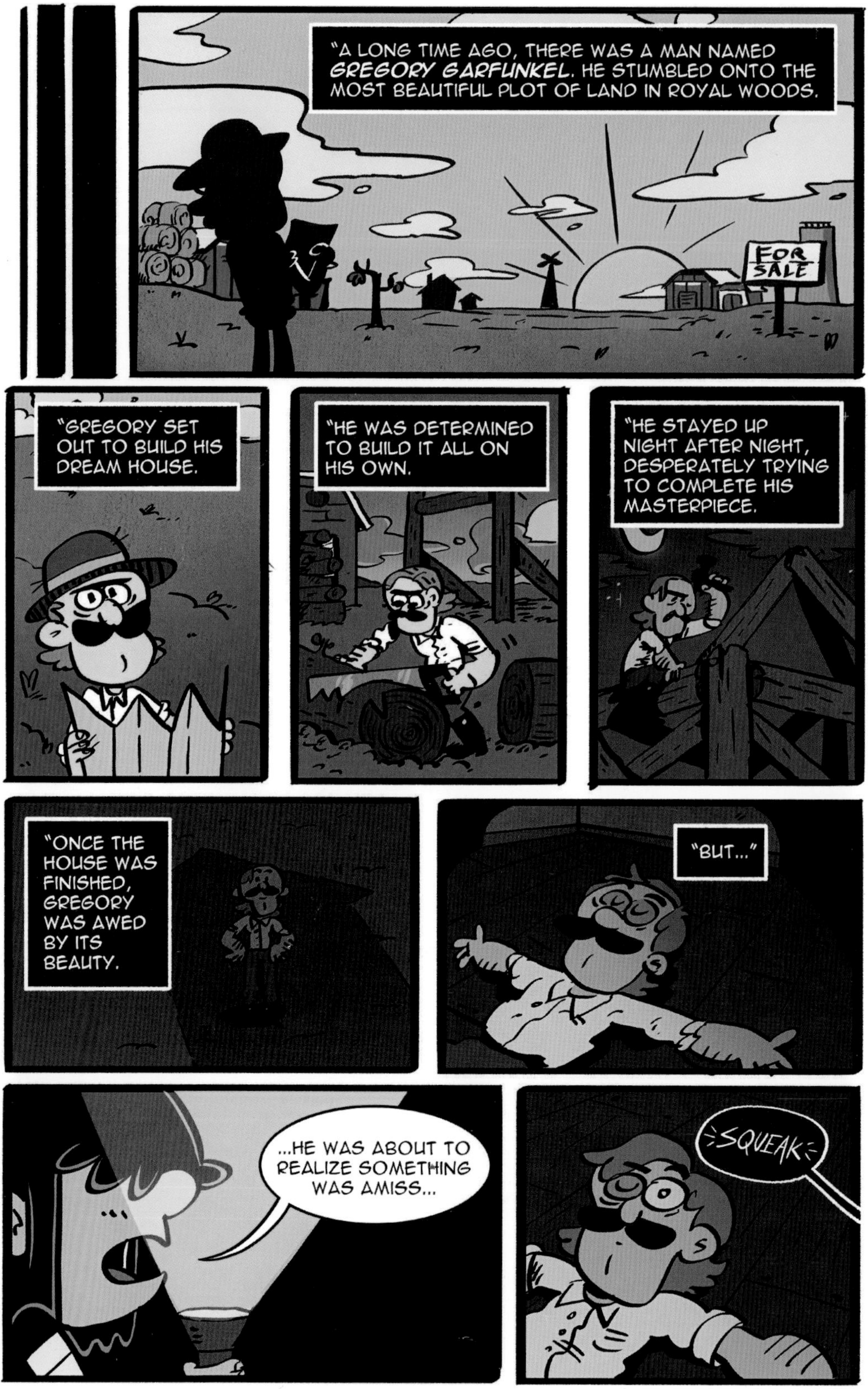
"A LONG TIME AGO, THERE WAS A MAN NAMED GREGORY GARFUNKEL. HE STUMBLED ONTO THE MOST BEAUTIFUL PLOT OF LAND IN ROYAL WOODS.
FOR SALE
"GREGORY SET OUT TO BUILD HIS DREAM HOUSE.
"HE WAS DETERMINED TO BUILD IT ALL ON HIS OWN.
"HE STAYED UP NIGHT AFTER NIGHT, DESPERATELY TRYING TO COMPLETE HIS MASTERPIECE.
"ONCE THE HOUSE WAS FINISHED, GREGORY WAS AWED BY ITS BEAUTY.
"BUT..."
...HE WAS ABOUT TO REALIZE SOMETHING WAS AMISS...
SQUEAK

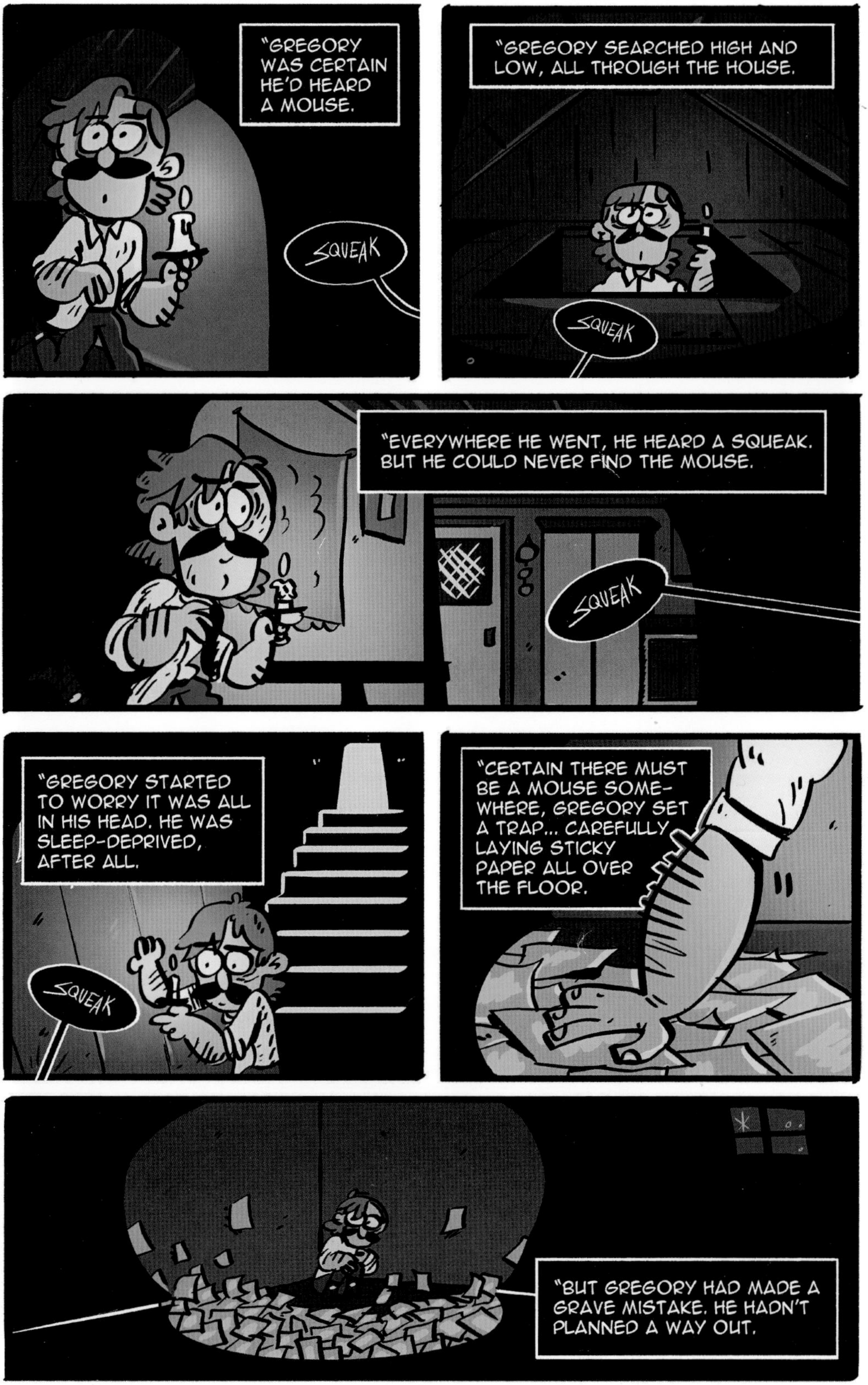
"GREGORY WAS CERTAIN HE'D HEARD A MOUSE.
SQUEAK
"GREGORY SEARCHED HIGH AND LOW, ALL THROUGH THE HOUSE.
SQUEAK
"EVERYWHERE HE WENT, HE HEARD A SQUEAK. BUT HE COULD NEVER FIND THE MOUSE.
SQUEAK
"GREGORY STARTED TO WORRY IT WAS ALL IN HIS HEAD. HE WAS SLEEP-DEPRIVED, AFTER ALL.
SQUEAK
"CERTAIN THERE MUST BE A MOUSE SOME-WHERE, GREGORY SET A TRAP... CAREFULLY LAYING STICKY PAPER ALL OVER THE FLOOR.
"BUT GREGORY HAD MADE A GRAVE MISTAKE. HE HADN'T PLANNED A WAY OUT.

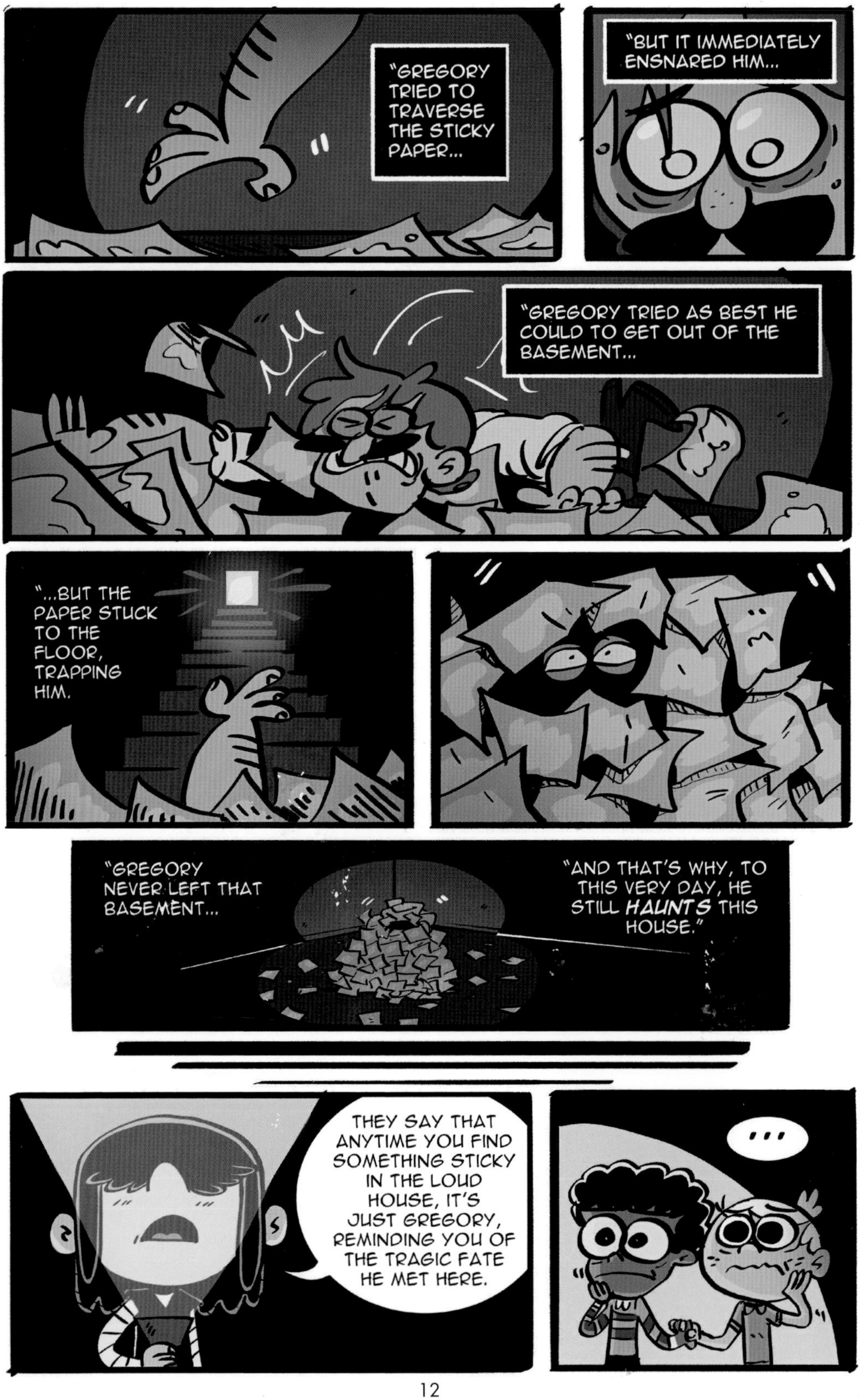
"GREGORY TRIED TO TRAVERSE THE STICKY PAPER...
"BUT IT IMMEDIATELY ENSNARED HIM...
"GREGORY TRIED AS BEST HE COULD TO GET OUT OF THE BASEMENT...
"...BUT THE PAPER STUCK TO THE FLOOR, TRAPPING HIM.
"GREGORY NEVER LEFT THAT BASEMENT...
"AND THAT'S WHY, TO THIS VERY DAY, HE STILL HAUNTS THIS HOUSE."
THEY SAY THAT ANYTIME YOU FIND SOMETHING STICKY IN THE LOUD HOUSE, IT'S JUST GREGORY, REMINDING YOU OF THE TRAGIC FATE HE MET HERE.
...

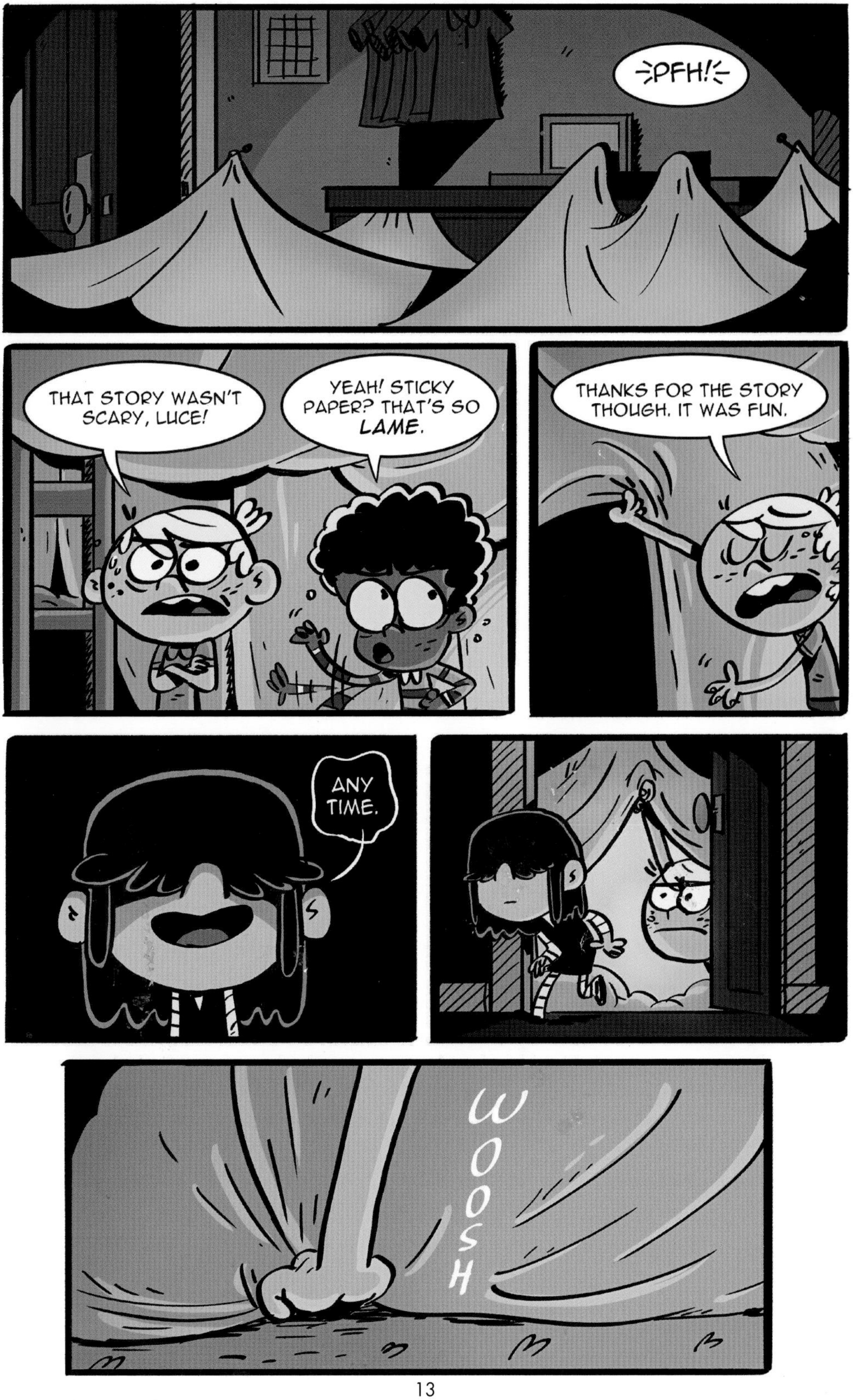
PFH!
THAT STORY WASN'T SCARY, LUCE!
YEAH! STICKY PAPER? THAT'S SO **LAME**.
THANKS FOR THE STORY THOUGH. IT WAS FUN.
ANY TIME.
WOOOSH

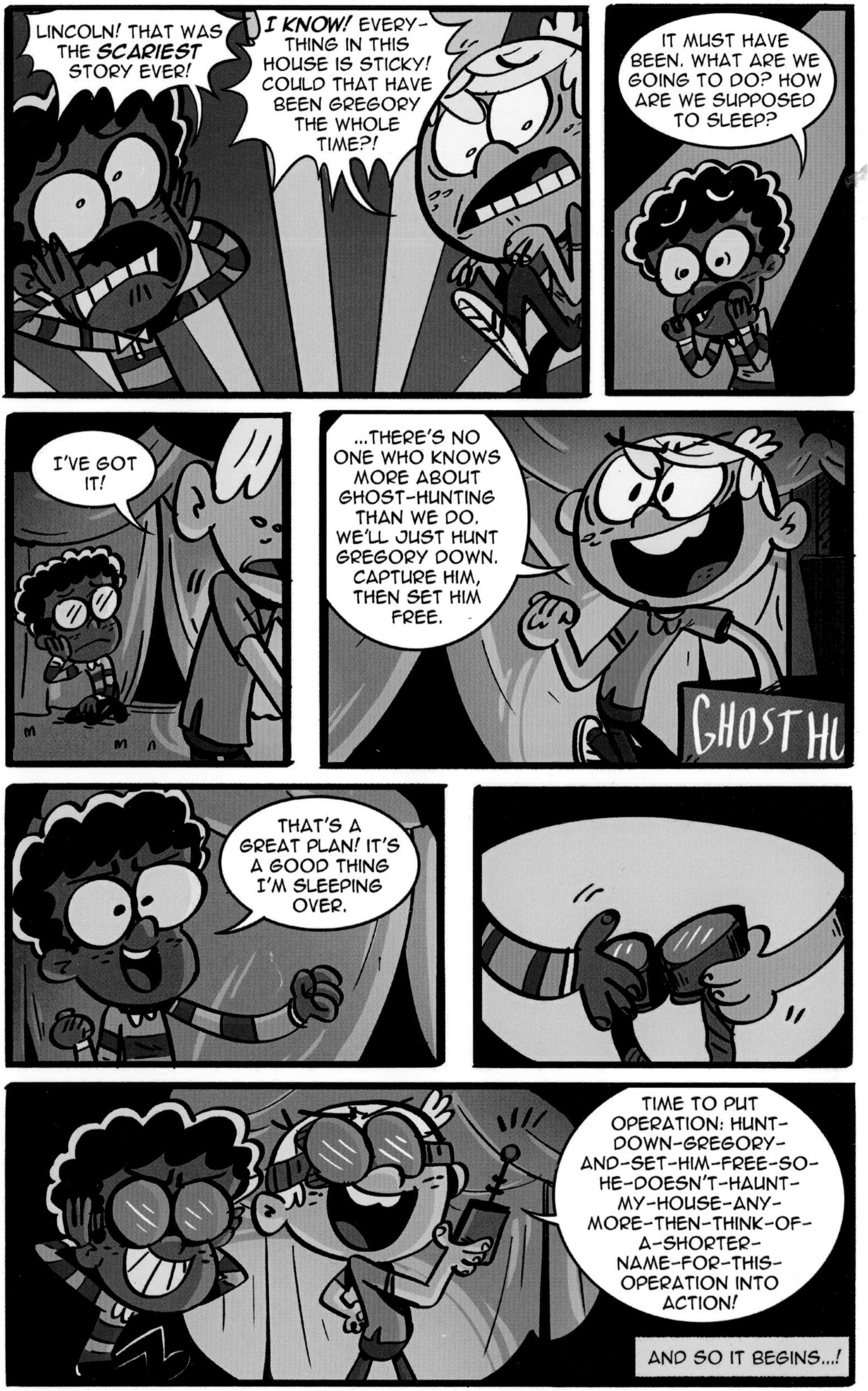
LINCOLN! THAT WAS THE SCARIEST STORY EVER!
I KNOW! EVERY-THING IN THIS HOUSE IS STICKY! COULD THAT HAVE BEEN GREGORY THE WHOLE TIME?!
IT MUST HAVE BEEN. WHAT ARE WE GOING TO DO? HOW ARE WE SUPPOSED TO SLEEP?
I'VE GOT IT!
...THERE'S NO ONE WHO KNOWS MORE ABOUT GHOST-HUNTING THAN WE DO. WE'LL JUST HUNT GREGORY DOWN. CAPTURE HIM, THEN SET HIM FREE.
GHOST HU
THAT'S A GREAT PLAN! IT'S A GOOD THING I'M SLEEPING OVER.
TIME TO PUT OPERATION: HUNT-DOWN-GREGORY-AND-SET-HIM-FREE-SO-HE-DOESN'T-HAUNT-MY-HOUSE-ANY-MORE-THEN-THINK-OF-A-SHORTER-NAME-FOR-THIS-OPERATION INTO ACTION!
AND SO IT BEGINS...!

"11:00 PM: DRAWING A PRANK"

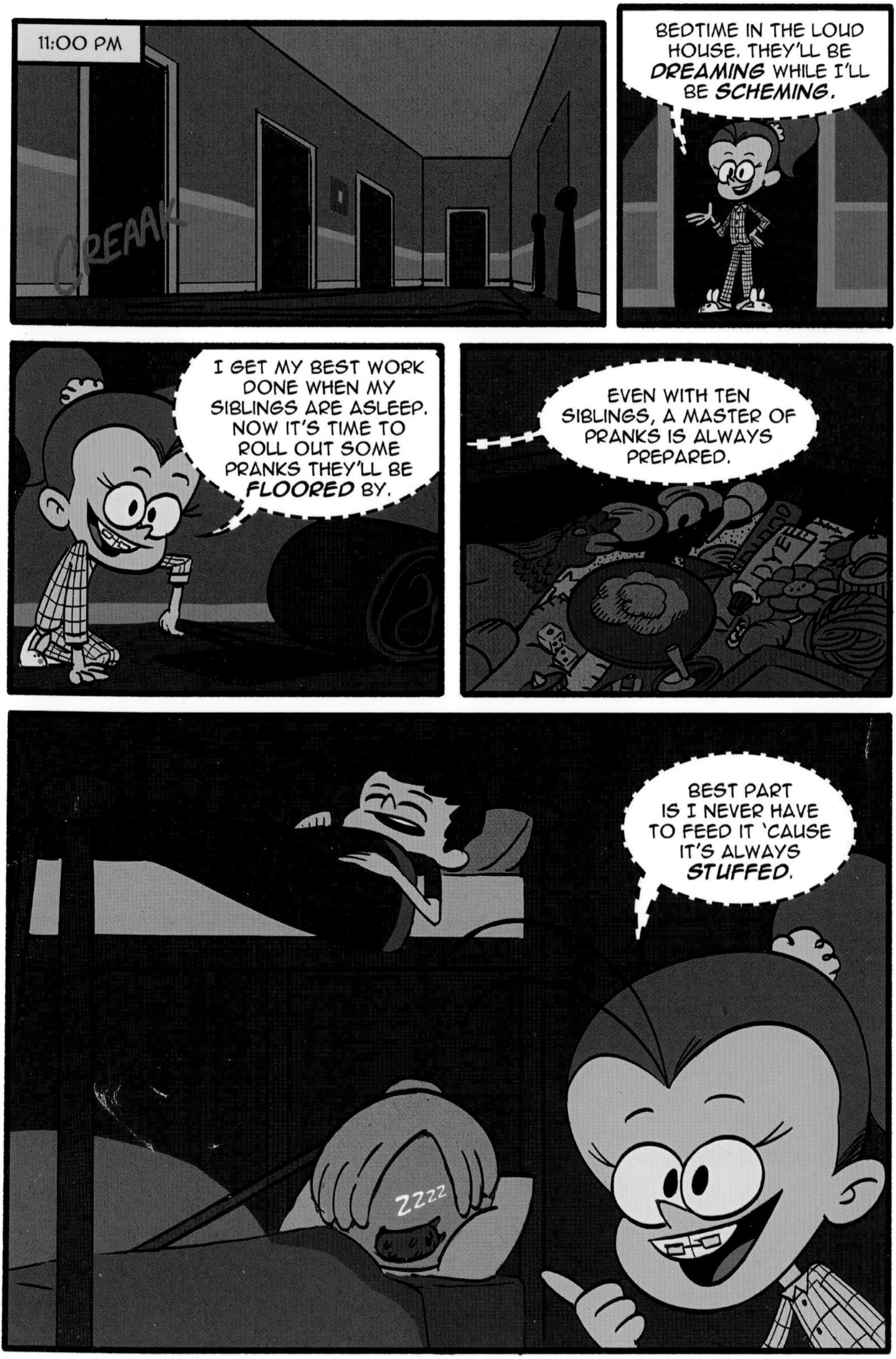
11:00 PM
CREAAK
BEDTIME IN THE LOUD HOUSE. THEY'LL BE DREAMING WHILE I'LL BE SCHEMING.
I GET MY BEST WORK DONE WHEN MY SIBLINGS ARE ASLEEP. NOW IT'S TIME TO ROLL OUT SOME PRANKS THEY'LL BE FLOORED BY.
EVEN WITH TEN SIBLINGS, A MASTER OF PRANKS IS ALWAYS PREPARED.
DYE
BEST PART IS I NEVER HAVE TO FEED IT 'CAUSE IT'S ALWAYS STUFFED.
ZZZZ

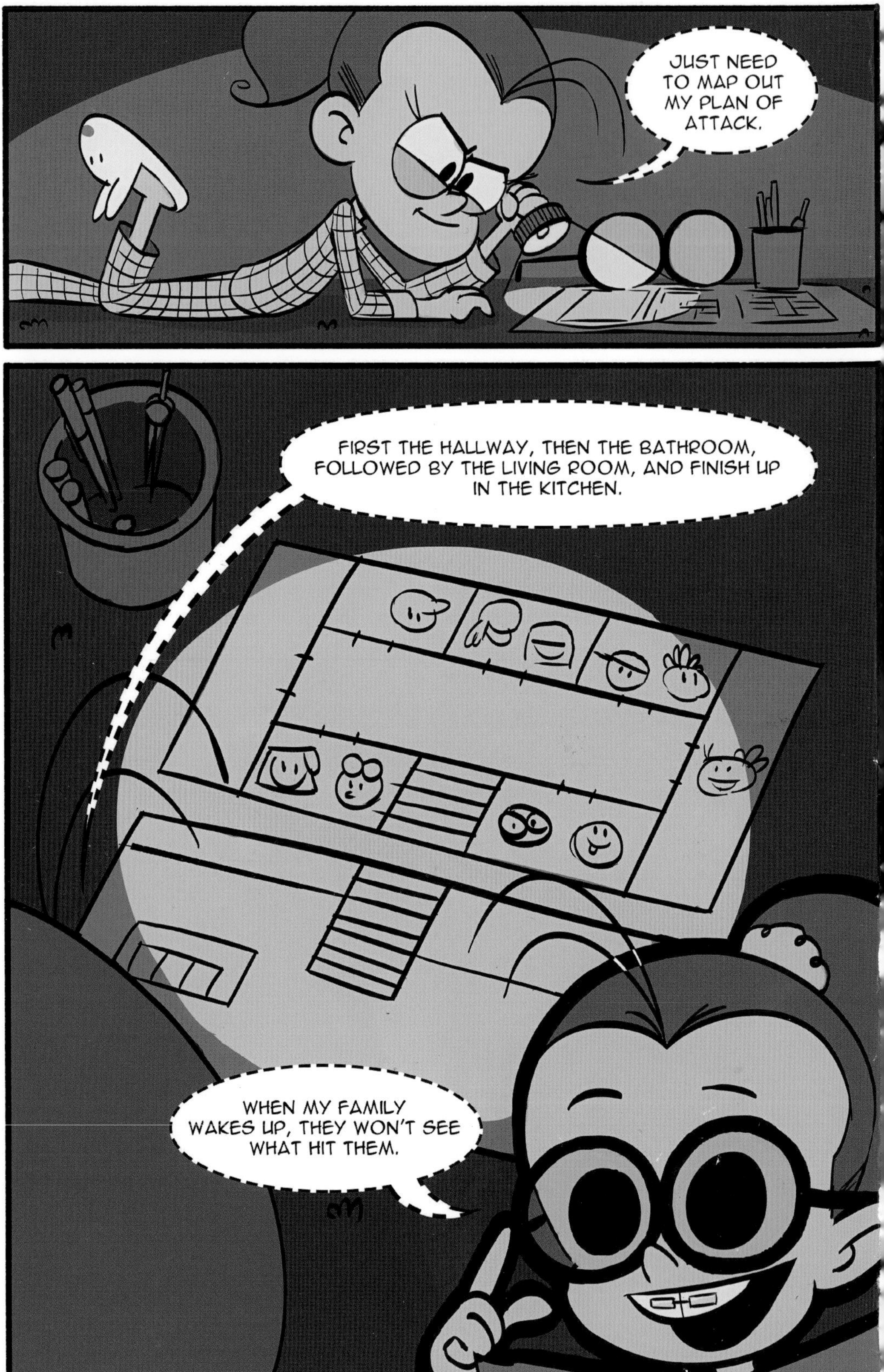
JUST NEED TO MAP OUT MY PLAN OF ATTACK.
FIRST THE HALLWAY, THEN THE BATHROOM, FOLLOWED BY THE LIVING ROOM, AND FINISH UP IN THE KITCHEN.
WHEN MY FAMILY WAKES UP, THEY WON'T SEE WHAT HIT THEM.

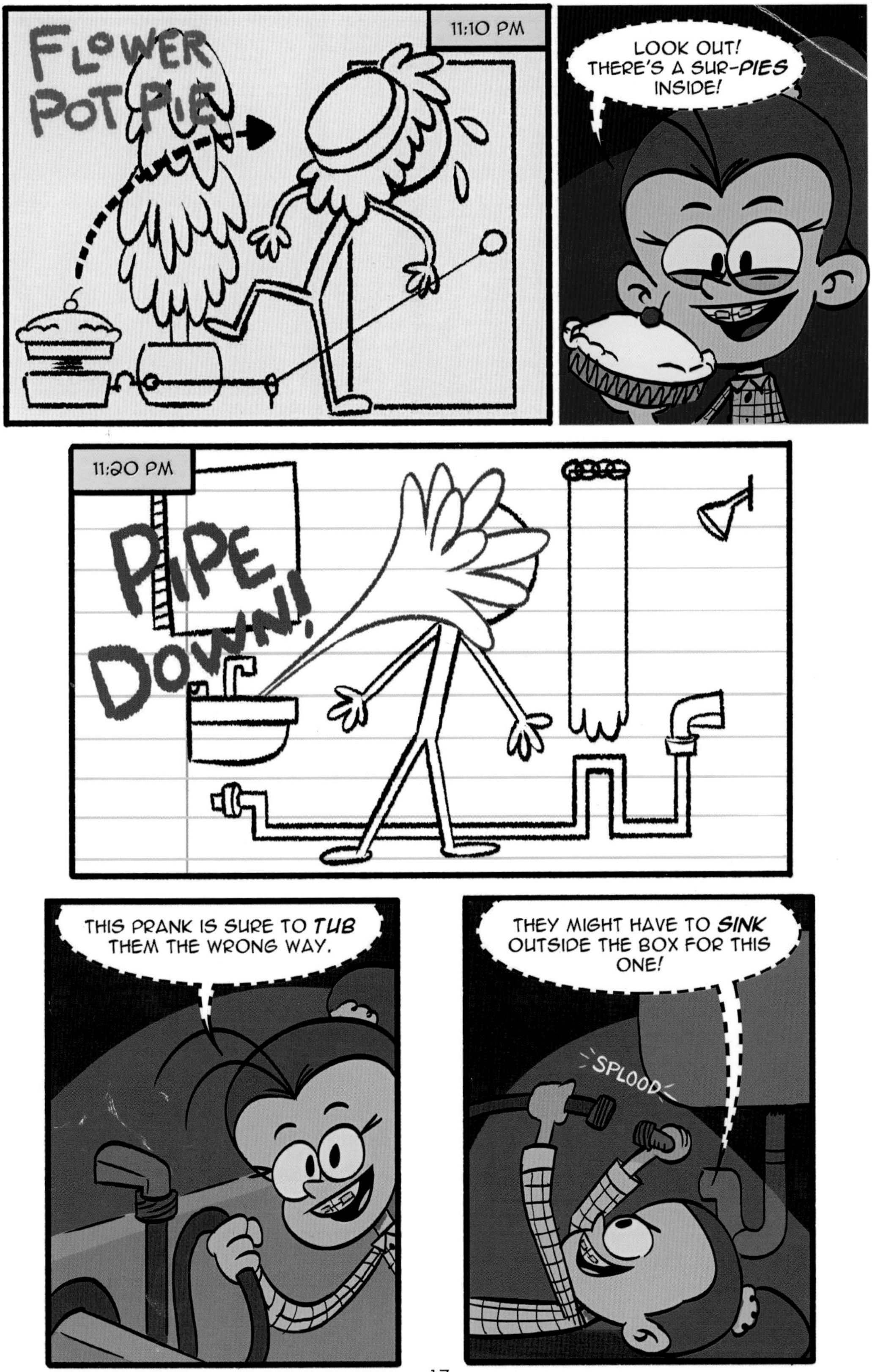
11:10 PM
FLOWER POT PIE
LOOK OUT! THERE'S A SUR-PIES INSIDE!
11:20 PM
PIPE DOWN!
THIS PRANK IS SURE TO TUB THEM THE WRONG WAY.
THEY MIGHT HAVE TO SINK OUTSIDE THE BOX FOR THIS ONE!
SPLOOD

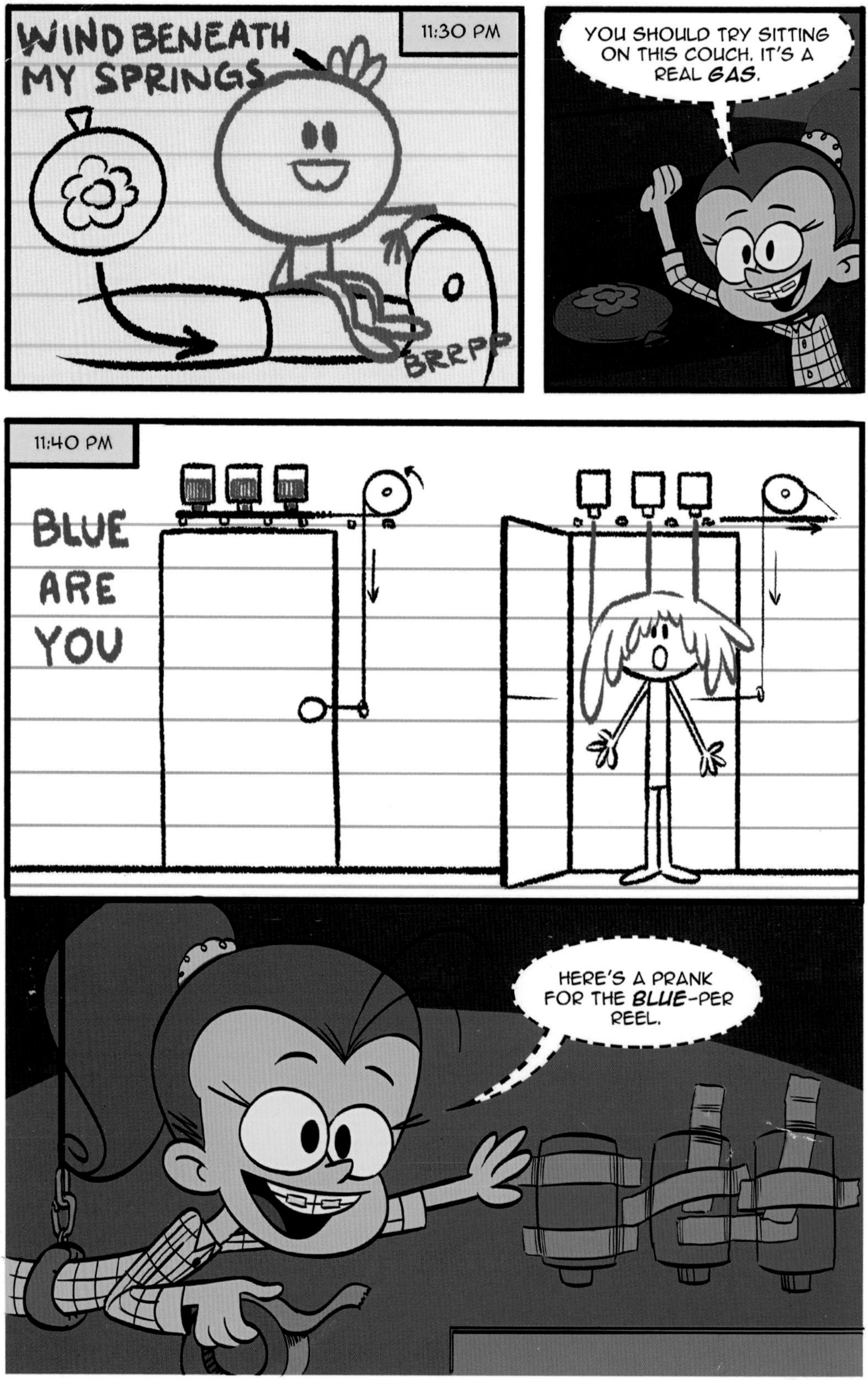

WIND BENEATH MY SPRINGS
11:30 PM
BRRPP
YOU SHOULD TRY SITTING ON THIS COUCH. IT'S A REAL GAS.
11:40 PM
BLUE ARE YOU
HERE'S A PRANK FOR THE BLUE-PER REEL.

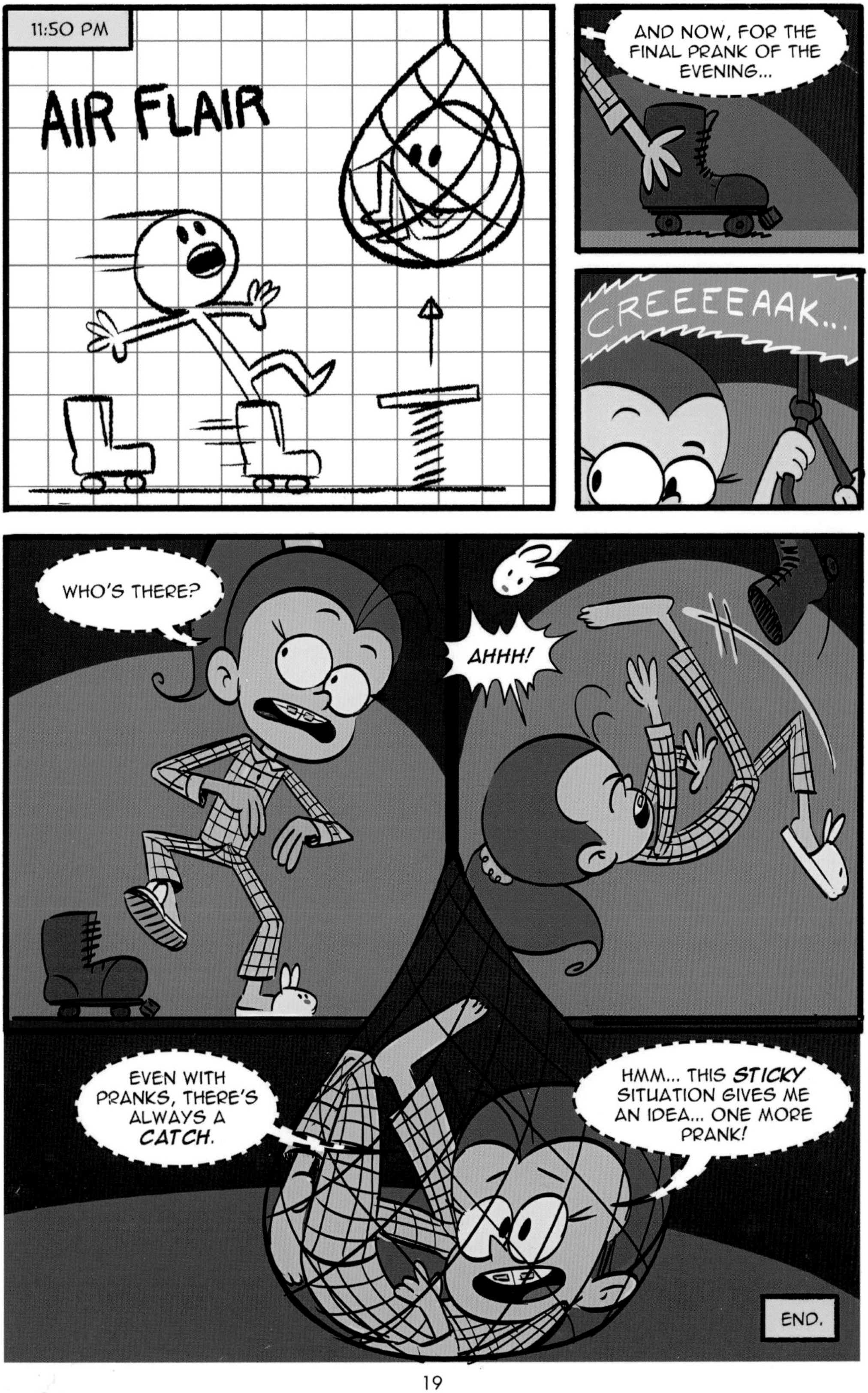
11:50 PM
AIR FLAIR
AND NOW, FOR THE FINAL PRANK OF THE EVENING...
CREEEEAAK...
WHO'S THERE?
AHHH!
EVEN WITH PRANKS, THERE'S ALWAYS A CATCH.
HMM... THIS STICKY SITUATION GIVES ME AN IDEA... ONE MORE PRANK!
END.

"12:00 AM: MIDNIGHT MELODY"

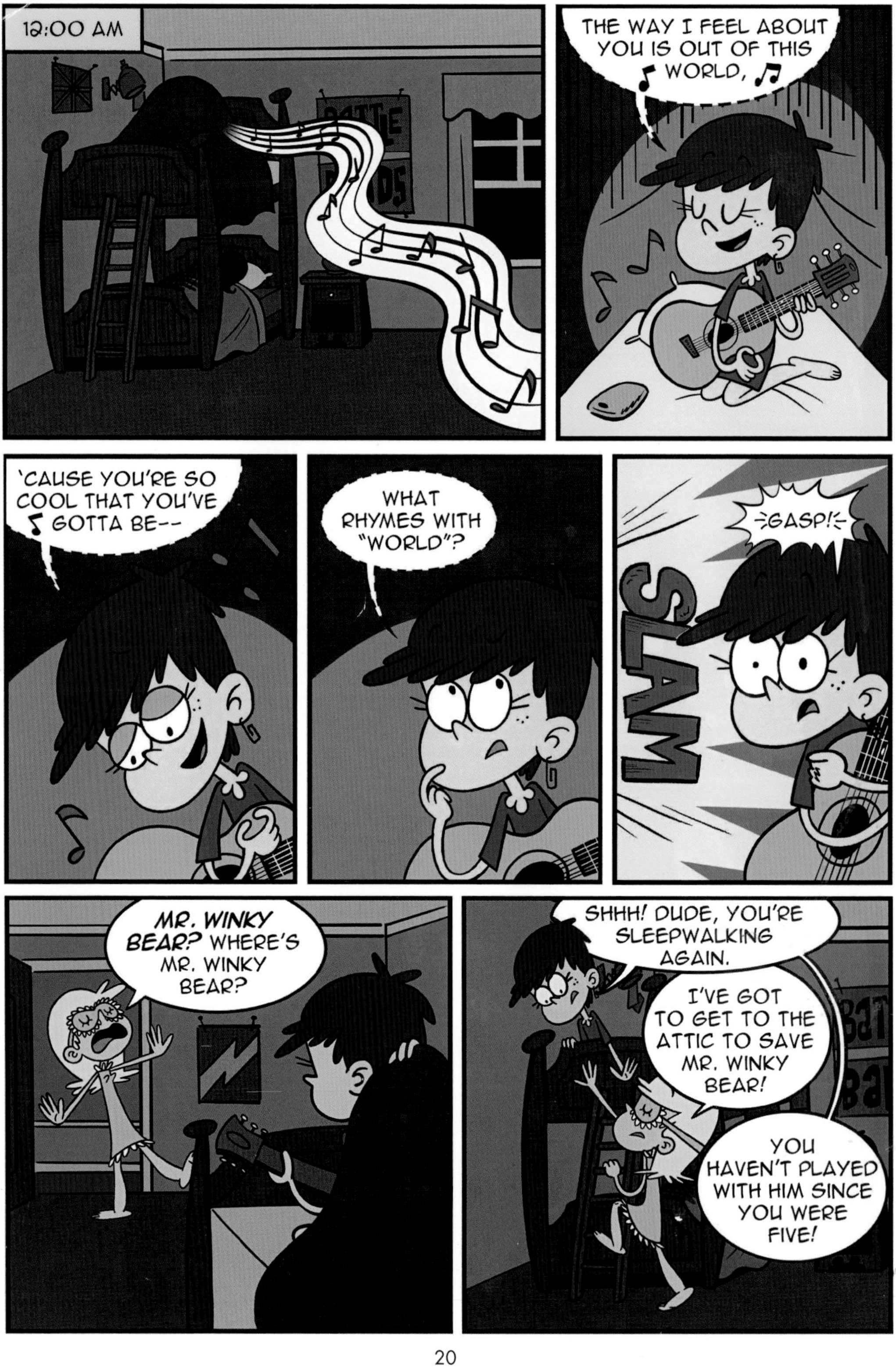
12:00 AM
THE WAY I FEEL ABOUT YOU IS OUT OF THIS WORLD,
'CAUSE YOU'RE SO COOL THAT YOU'VE GOTTA BE--
WHAT RHYMES WITH "WORLD"?
GASP!
SLAM
MR. WINKY BEAR? WHERE'S MR. WINKY BEAR?
SHHH! DUDE, YOU'RE SLEEPWALKING AGAIN.
I'VE GOT TO GET TO THE ATTIC TO SAVE MR. WINKY BEAR!
YOU HAVEN'T PLAYED WITH HIM SINCE YOU WERE FIVE!

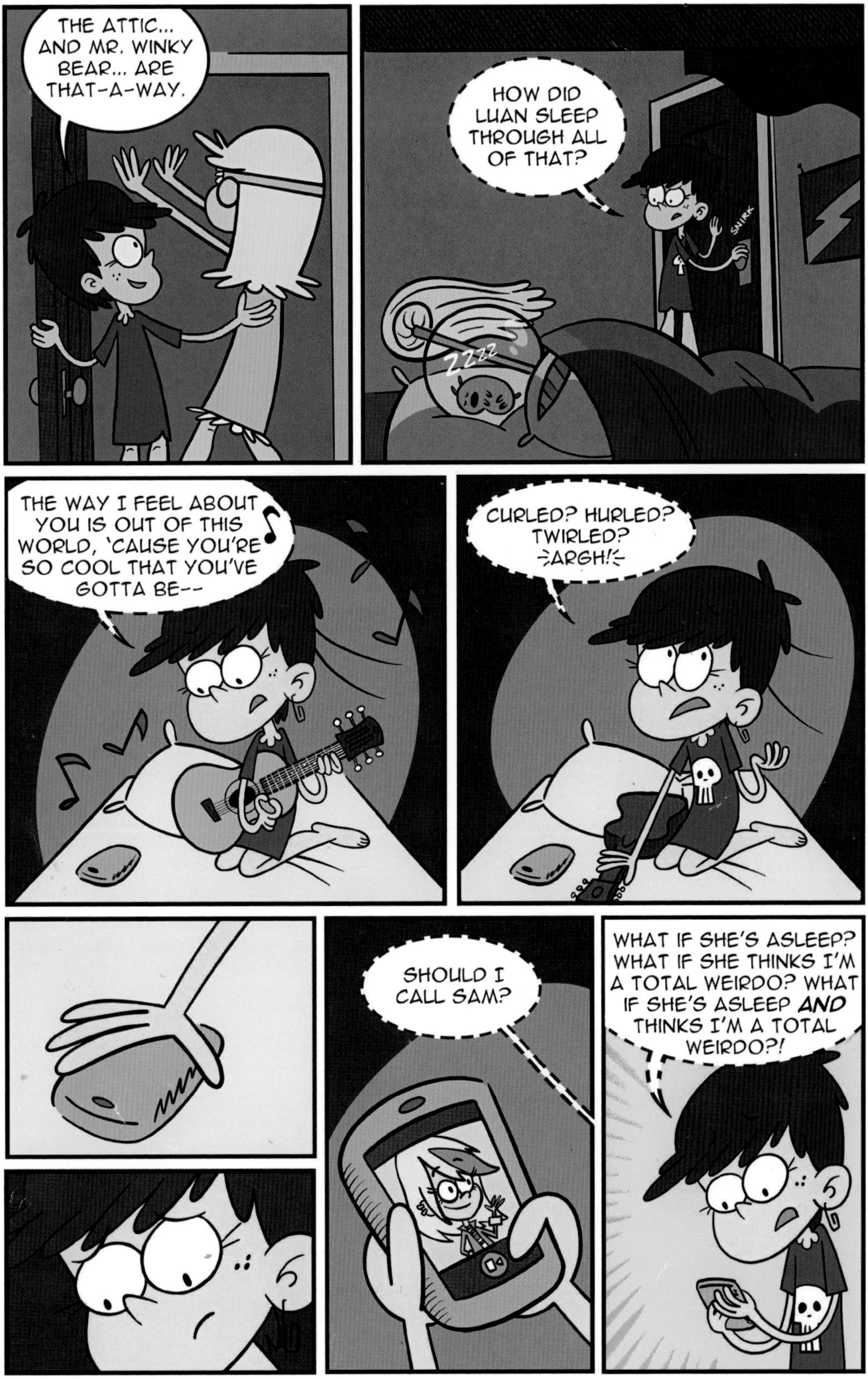
THE ATTIC... AND MR. WINKY BEAR... ARE THAT-A-WAY.
HOW DID LUAN SLEEP THROUGH ALL OF THAT?
SNIRK
ZZZZ
THE WAY I FEEL ABOUT YOU IS OUT OF THIS WORLD, 'CAUSE YOU'RE SO COOL THAT YOU'VE GOTTA BE--
CURLED? HURLED? TWIRLED? ARGH!
SHOULD I CALL SAM?
WHAT IF SHE'S ASLEEP? WHAT IF SHE THINKS I'M A TOTAL WEIRDO? WHAT IF SHE'S ASLEEP AND THINKS I'M A TOTAL WEIRDO?!

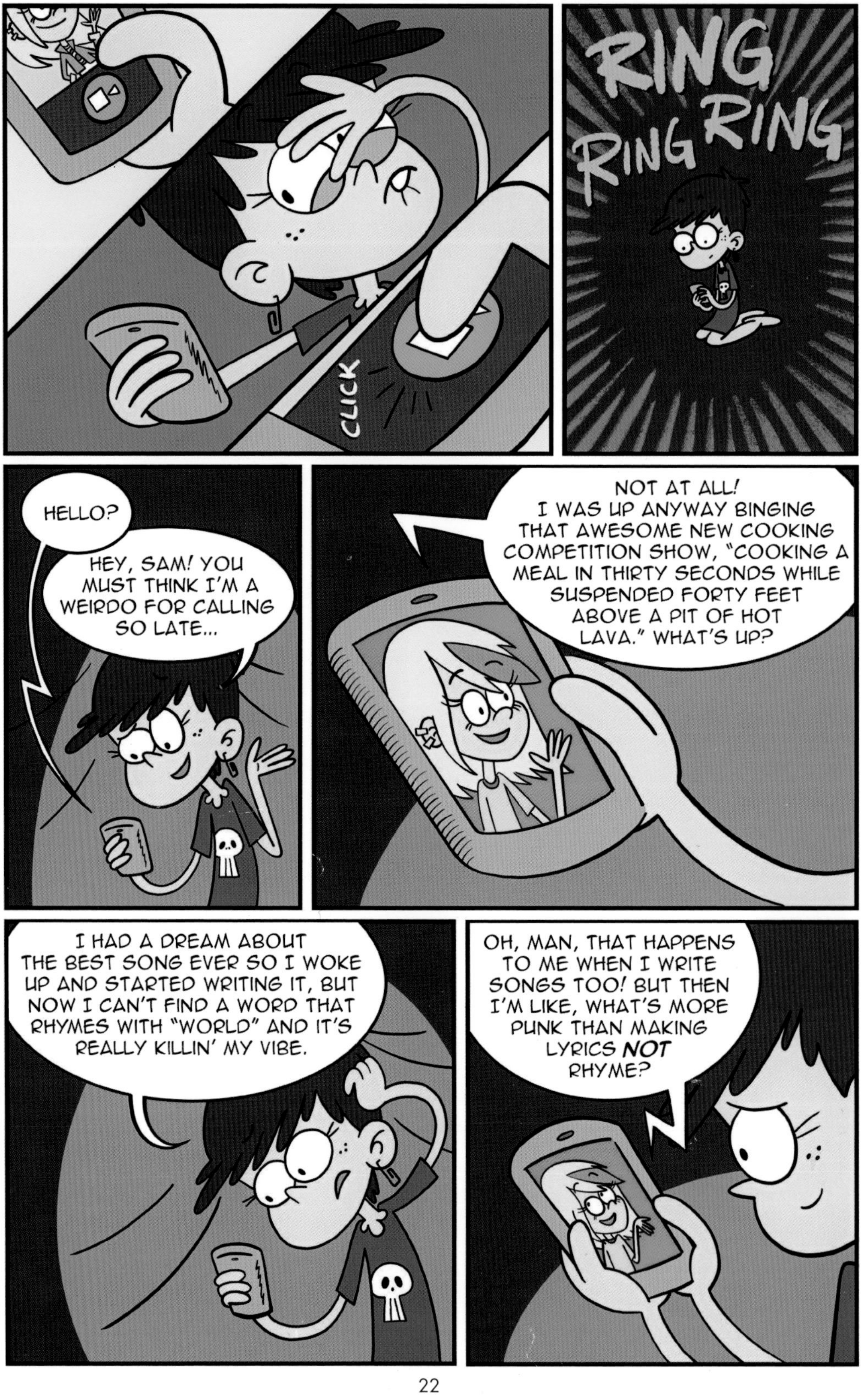
CLICK
RING
RING RING
HELLO?
HEY, SAM! YOU MUST THINK I'M A WEIRDO FOR CALLING SO LATE...
NOT AT ALL! I WAS UP ANYWAY BINGING THAT AWESOME NEW COOKING COMPETITION SHOW, "COOKING A MEAL IN THIRTY SECONDS WHILE SUSPENDED FORTY FEET ABOVE A PIT OF HOT LAVA." WHAT'S UP?
I HAD A DREAM ABOUT THE BEST SONG EVER SO I WOKE UP AND STARTED WRITING IT, BUT NOW I CAN'T FIND A WORD THAT RHYMES WITH "WORLD" AND IT'S REALLY KILLIN' MY VIBE.
OH, MAN, THAT HAPPENS TO ME WHEN I WRITE SONGS TOO! BUT THEN I'M LIKE, WHAT'S MORE PUNK THAN MAKING LYRICS ***NOT*** RHYME?

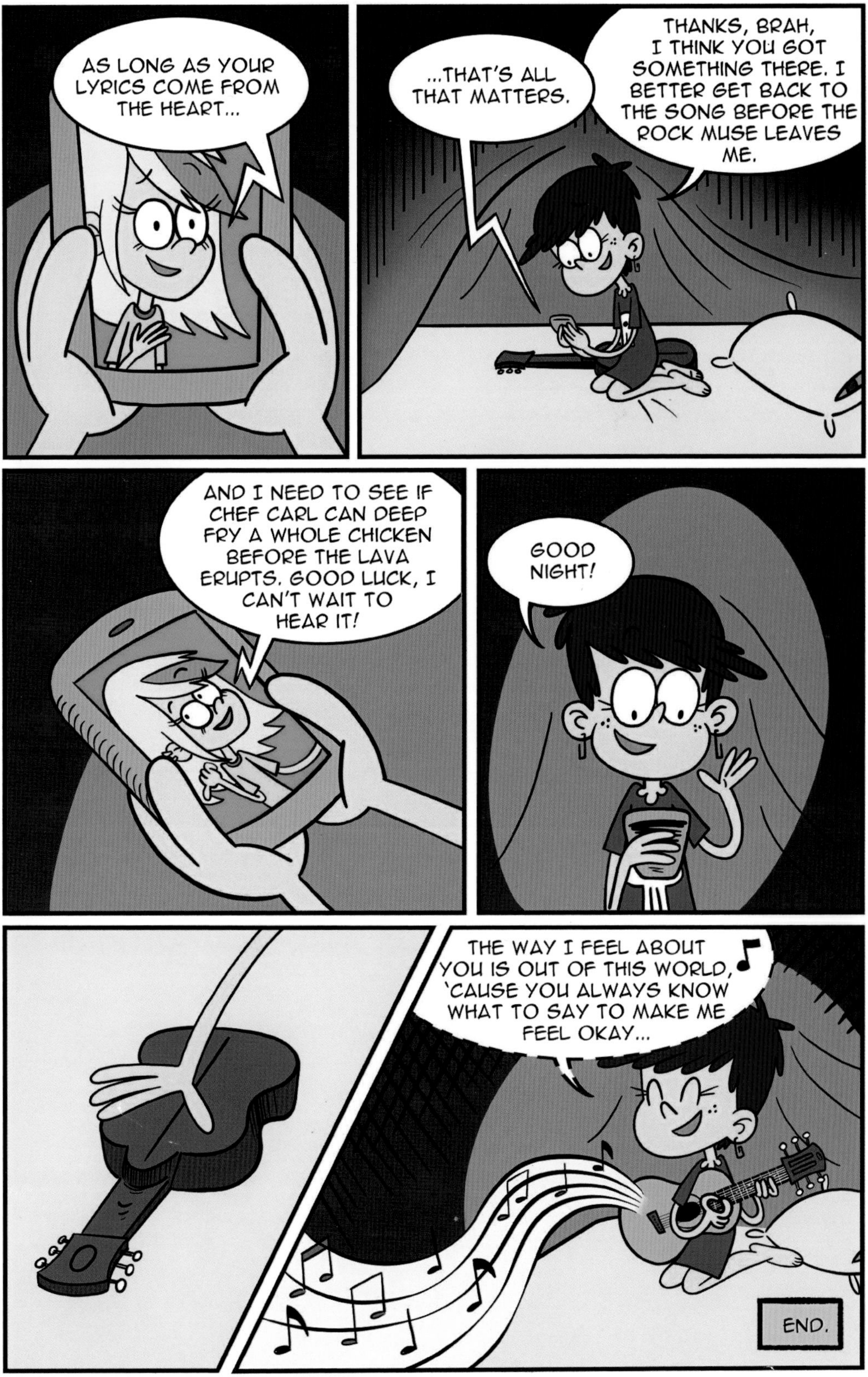
AS LONG AS YOUR LYRICS COME FROM THE HEART...
...THAT'S ALL THAT MATTERS.
THANKS, BRAH, I THINK YOU GOT SOMETHING THERE. I BETTER GET BACK TO THE SONG BEFORE THE ROCK MUSE LEAVES ME.
AND I NEED TO SEE IF CHEF CARL CAN DEEP FRY A WHOLE CHICKEN BEFORE THE LAVA ERUPTS. GOOD LUCK, I CAN'T WAIT TO HEAR IT!
GOOD NIGHT!
THE WAY I FEEL ABOUT YOU IS OUT OF THIS WORLD, 'CAUSE YOU ALWAYS KNOW WHAT TO SAY TO MAKE ME FEEL OKAY...
END.

"1:00 AM: GOAL-ORIENTED"

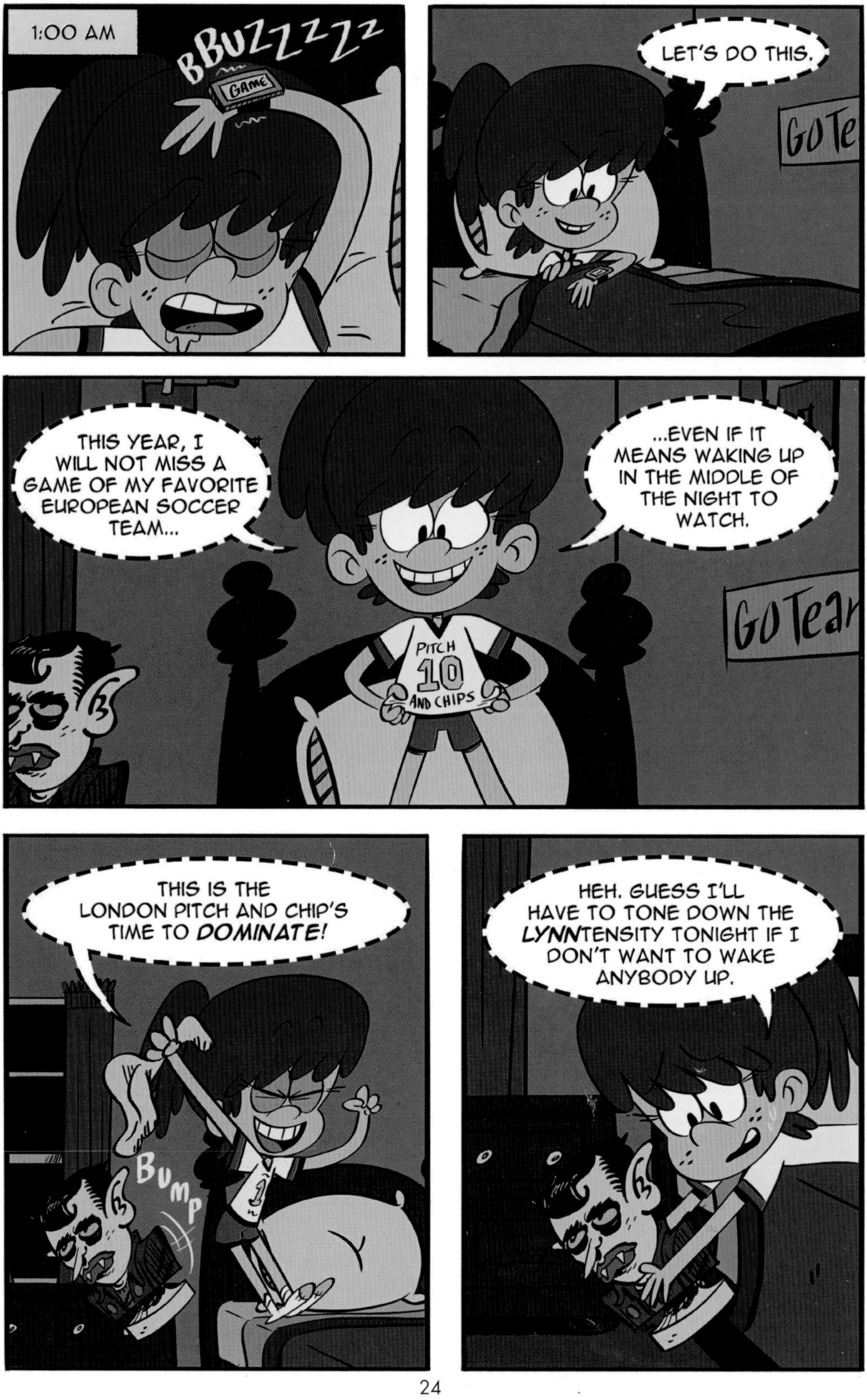
1:00 AM
BBUZZZZZ
GAME
LET'S DO THIS.
GO Te
THIS YEAR, I WILL NOT MISS A GAME OF MY FAVORITE EUROPEAN SOCCER TEAM...
...EVEN IF IT MEANS WAKING UP IN THE MIDDLE OF THE NIGHT TO WATCH.
GO Tea
PITCH 10 AND CHIPS
THIS IS THE LONDON PITCH AND CHIP'S TIME TO *DOMINATE*!
BUMP
HEH. GUESS I'LL HAVE TO TONE DOWN THE ***LYNN***TENSITY TONIGHT IF I DON'T WANT TO WAKE ANYBODY UP.

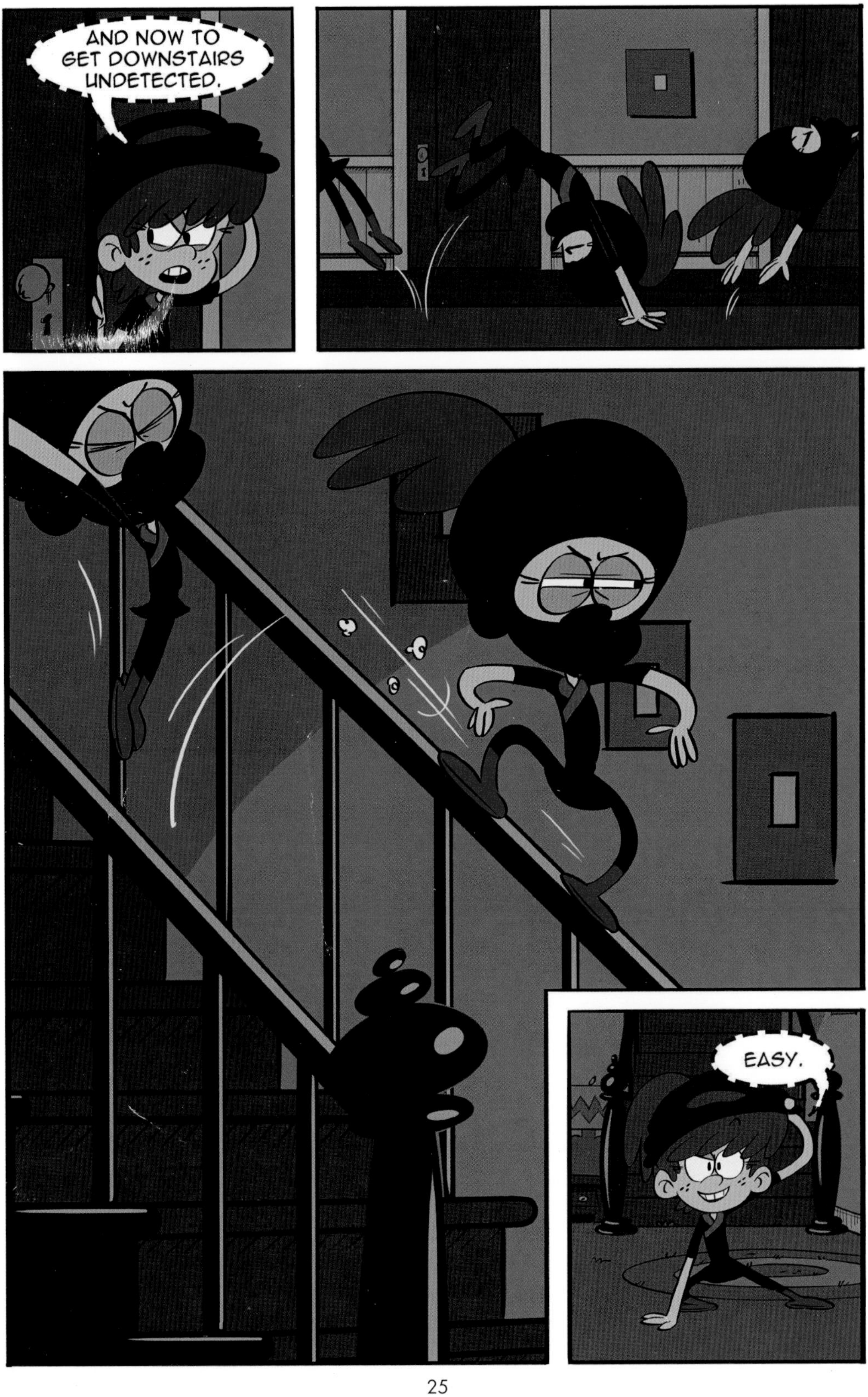
AND NOW TO GET DOWNSTAIRS UNDETECTED.
EASY.

HERE WE GO. NOT TOO LOUD.

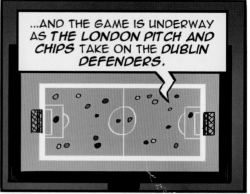

...AND THE GAME IS UNDERWAY AS *THE LONDON PITCH AND CHIPS* TAKE ON THE *DUBLIN DEFENDERS.*

1:10 AM

OH! THAT WAS A CLOSE ONE!

1:20 AM

THOSE AT HOME MUST BE *SCREAMING* WITH EXCITEMENT!

1:30 AM

AND THAT'S HALF! OUR TWO TEAMS ARE SCORELESS.

MMMF!

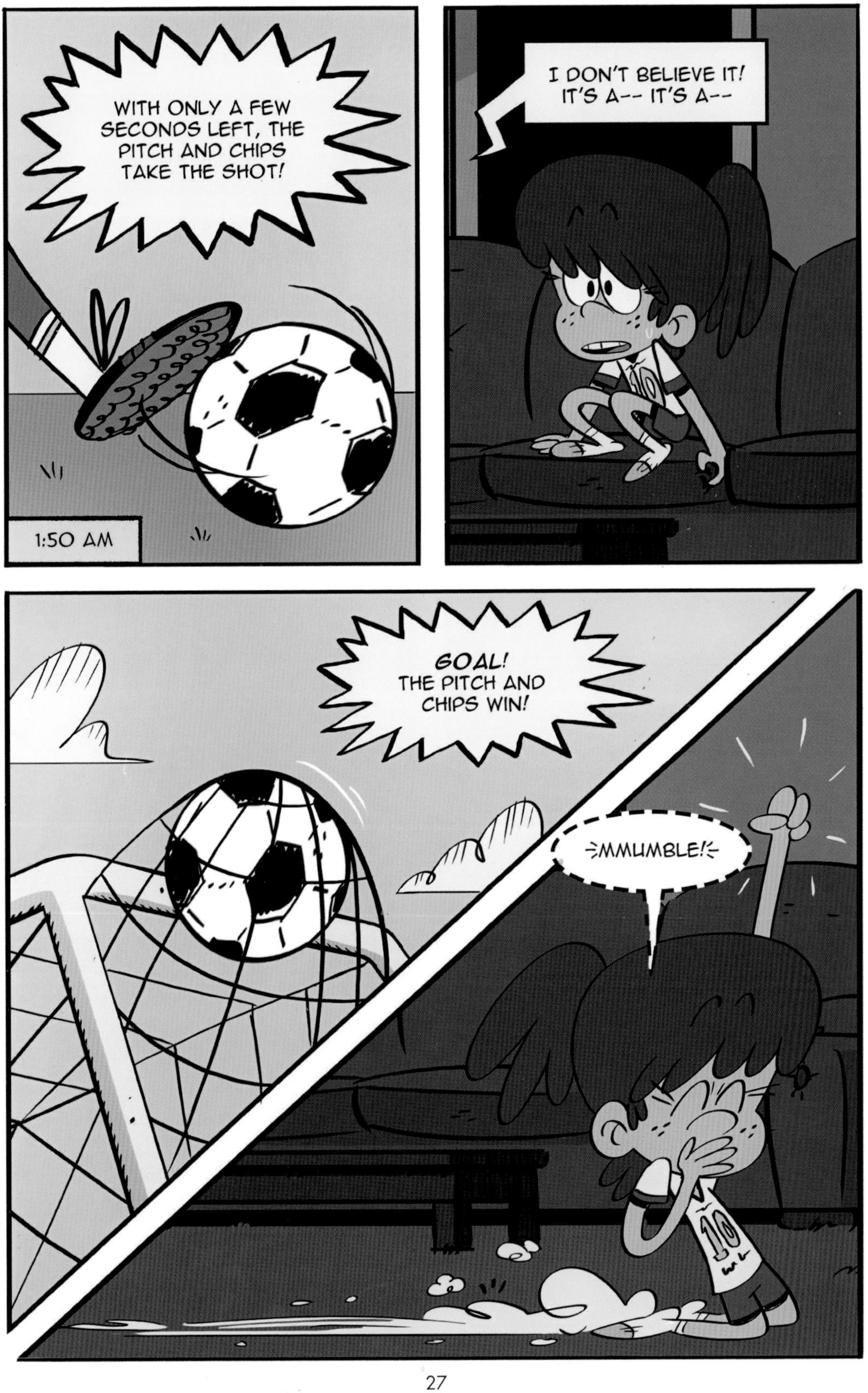
WITH ONLY A FEW SECONDS LEFT, THE PITCH AND CHIPS TAKE THE SHOT!
1:50 AM
I DON'T BELIEVE IT! IT'S A-- IT'S A--
GOAL! THE PITCH AND CHIPS WIN!
MMUMBLE!

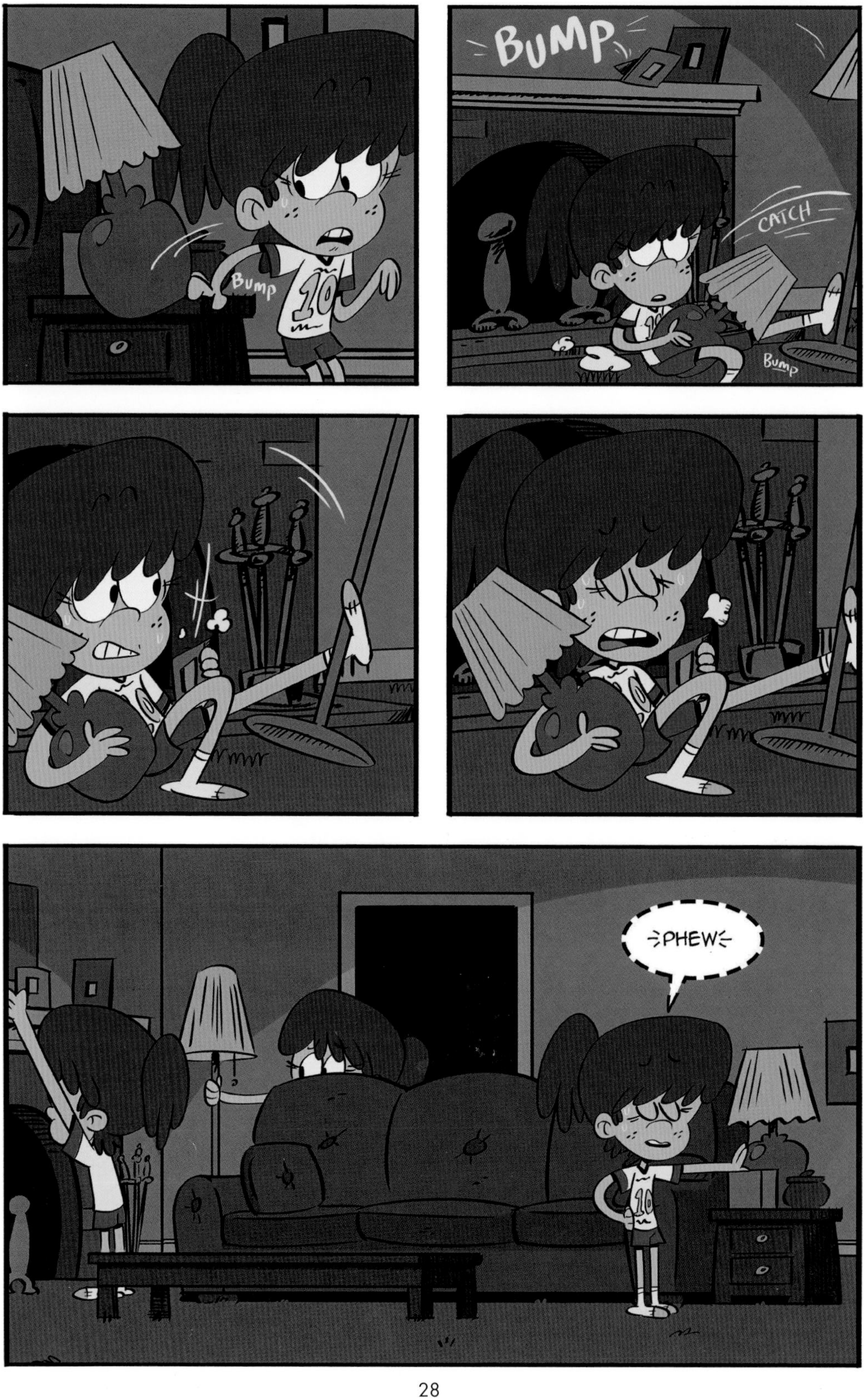
BUMP
BUMP
BUMP
CATCH
BUMP
PHEW

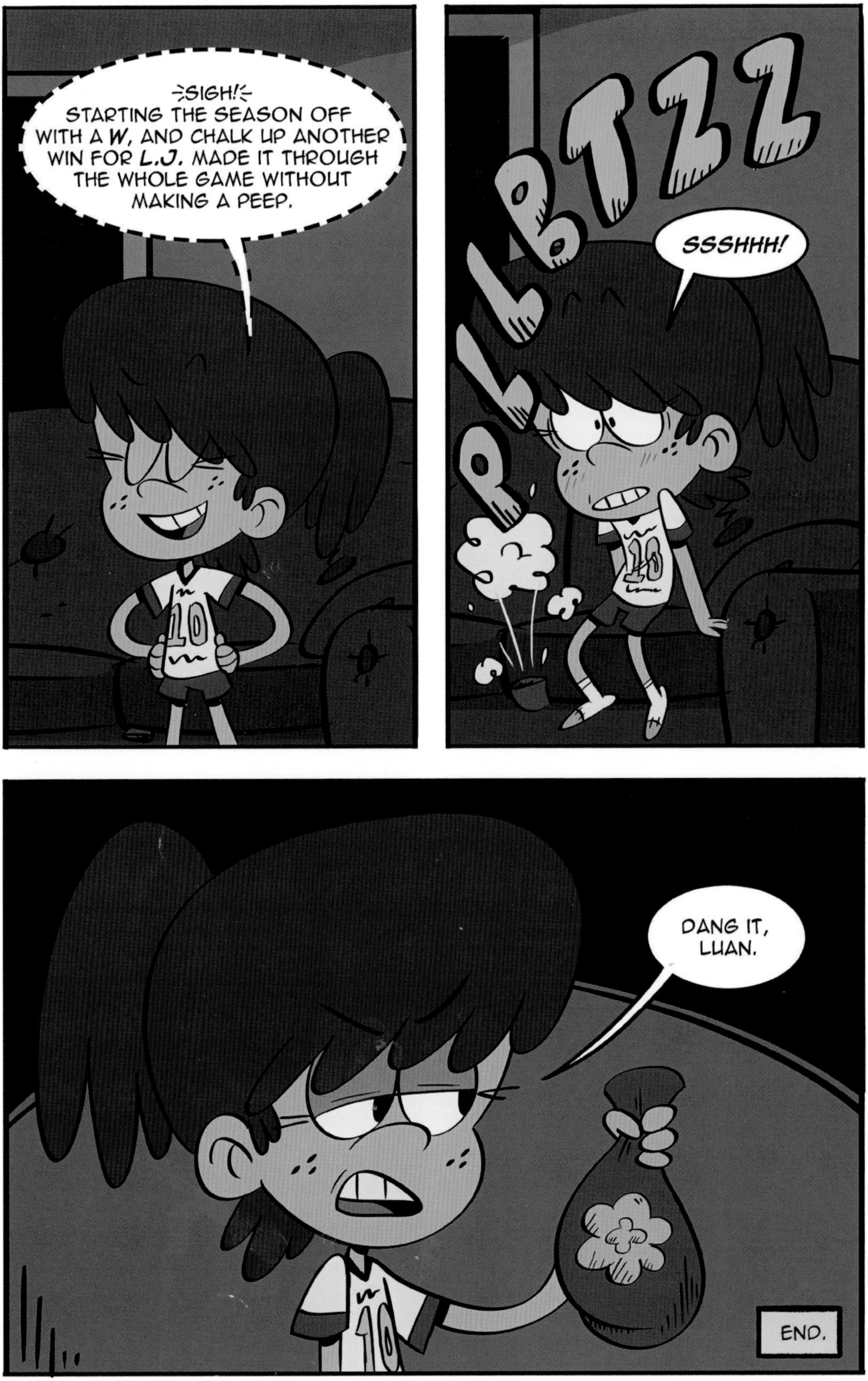
SIGH!
STARTING THE SEASON OFF WITH A W, AND CHALK UP ANOTHER WIN FOR L.J. MADE IT THROUGH THE WHOLE GAME WITHOUT MAKING A PEEP.
PLLBTZZZ
SSSHHH!
DANG IT, LUAN.
END.

"1:55 AM: GHOST IN THE BASEMENT"

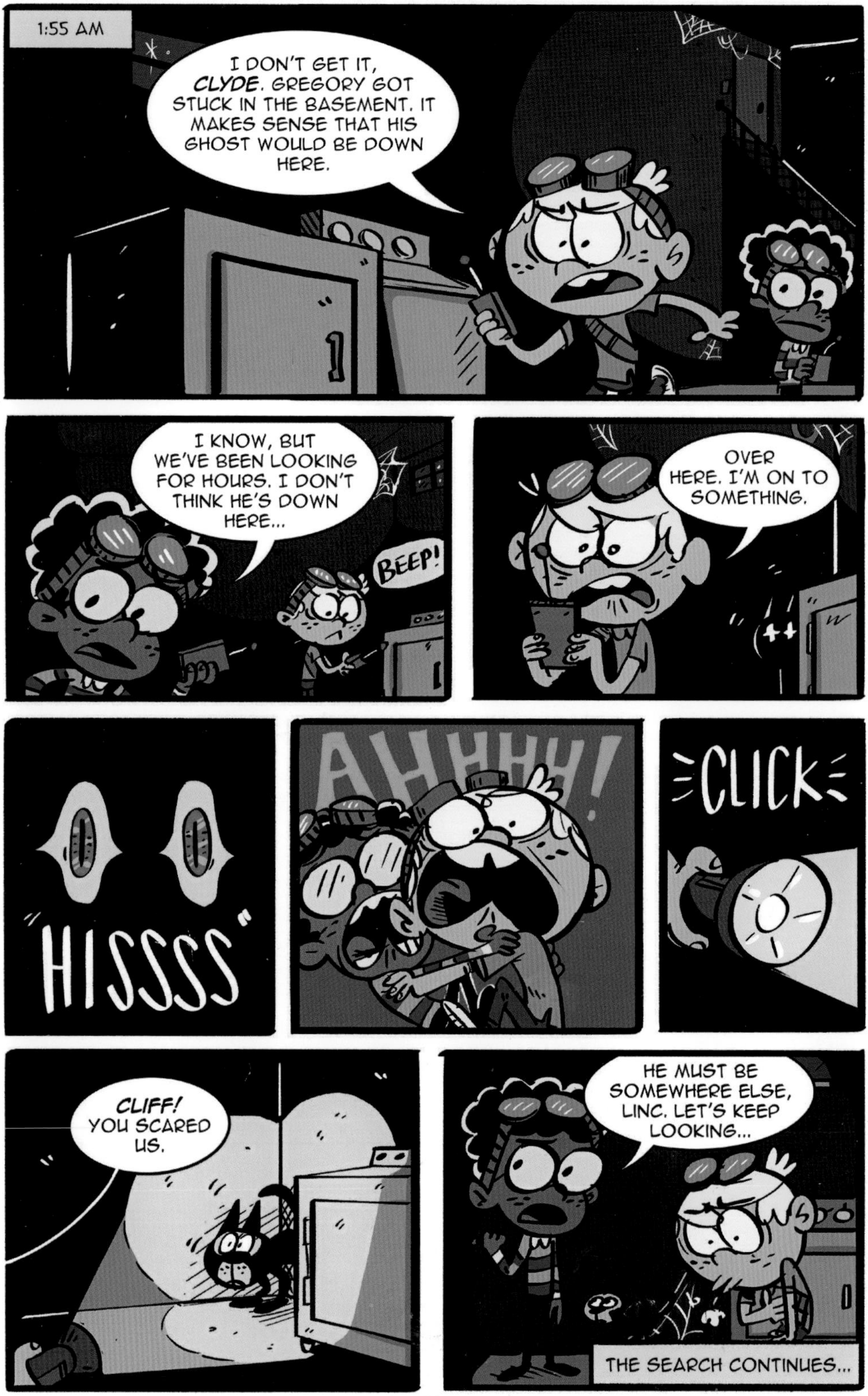

1:55 AM
I DON'T GET IT, *CLYDE*. GREGORY GOT STUCK IN THE BASEMENT. IT MAKES SENSE THAT HIS GHOST WOULD BE DOWN HERE.
I KNOW, BUT WE'VE BEEN LOOKING FOR HOURS. I DON'T THINK HE'S DOWN HERE...
BEEP!
OVER HERE. I'M ON TO SOMETHING.
"HISSSS"
AHHHH!
CLICK
CLIFF! YOU SCARED US.
HE MUST BE SOMEWHERE ELSE, LINC. LET'S KEEP LOOKING...
THE SEARCH CONTINUES...

"2:00 AM: THE EARLY BIRDS AND THE WORMS"

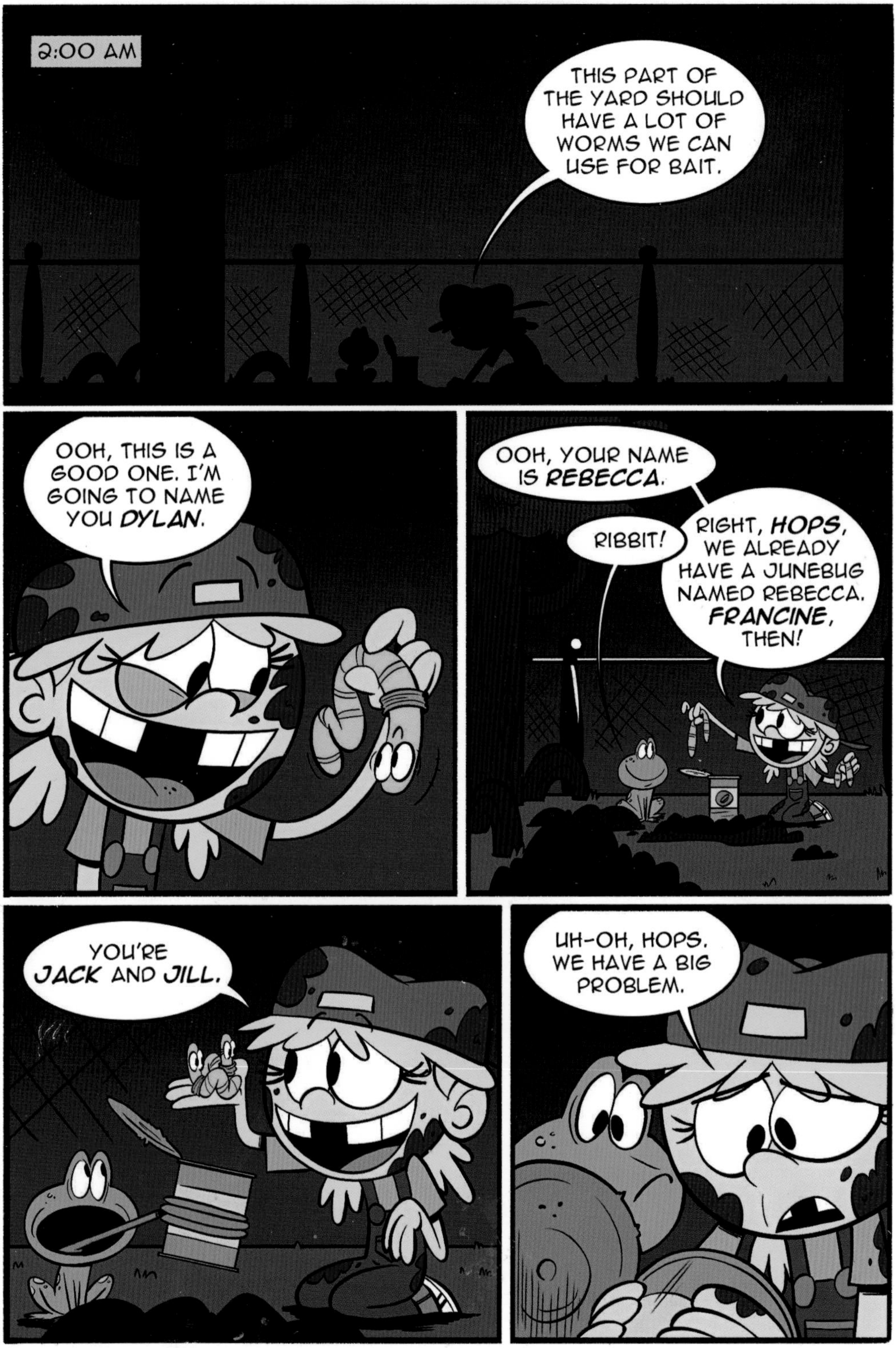
2:00 AM
THIS PART OF THE YARD SHOULD HAVE A LOT OF WORMS WE CAN USE FOR BAIT.
OOH, THIS IS A GOOD ONE. I'M GOING TO NAME YOU *DYLAN*.
OOH, YOUR NAME IS *REBECCA*.
RIBBIT!
RIGHT, *HOPS*, WE ALREADY HAVE A JUNEBUG NAMED REBECCA. *FRANCINE*, THEN!
YOU'RE *JACK* AND *JILL*.
UH-OH, HOPS. WE HAVE A BIG PROBLEM.

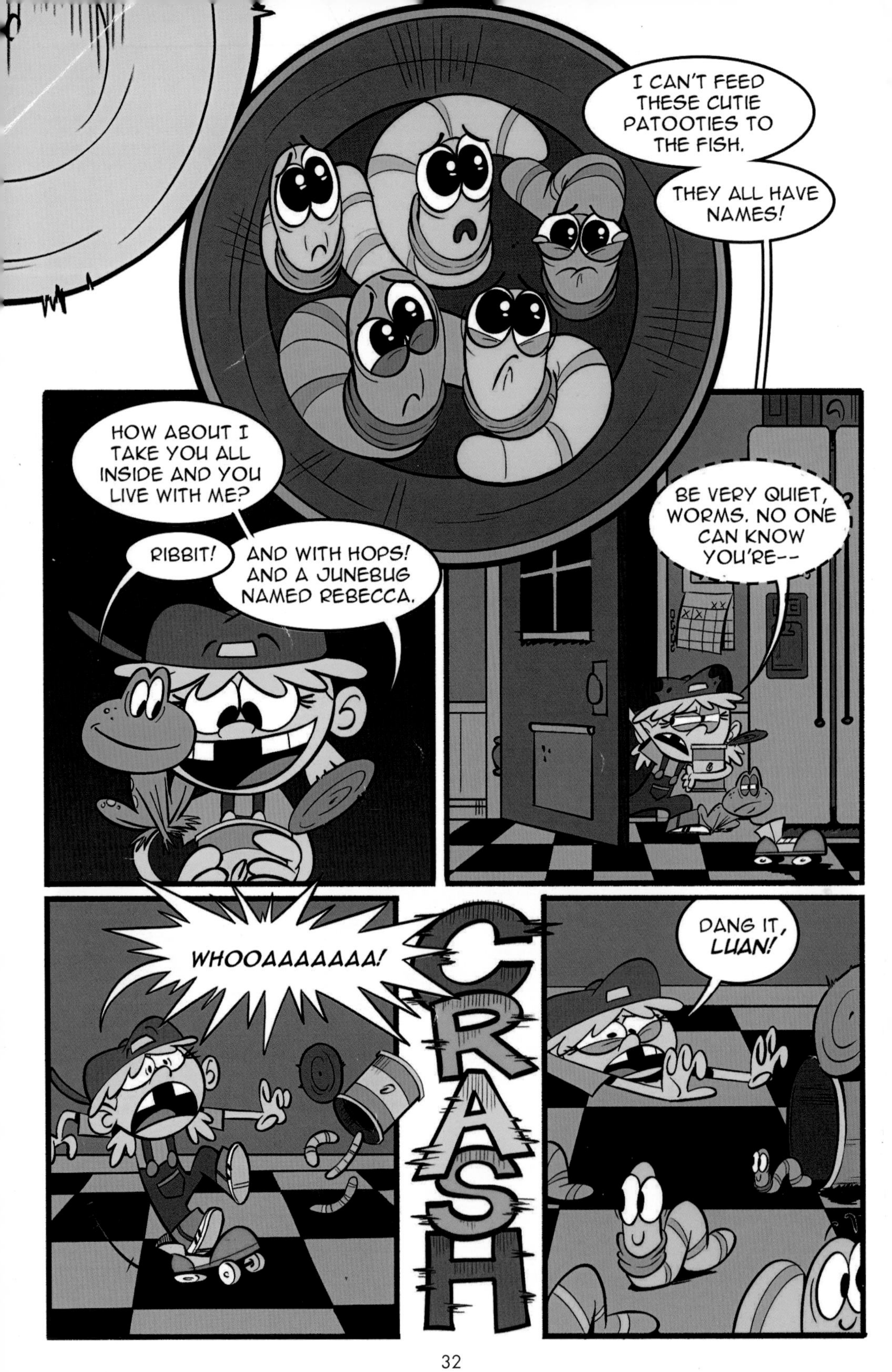
I CAN'T FEED THESE CUTIE PATOOTIES TO THE FISH.
THEY ALL HAVE NAMES!
HOW ABOUT I TAKE YOU ALL INSIDE AND YOU LIVE WITH ME?
RIBBIT!
AND WITH HOPS! AND A JUNEBUG NAMED REBECCA.
BE VERY QUIET, WORMS. NO ONE CAN KNOW YOU'RE--
WHOOAAAAAAAA!
CRASH
DANG IT, LUAN!

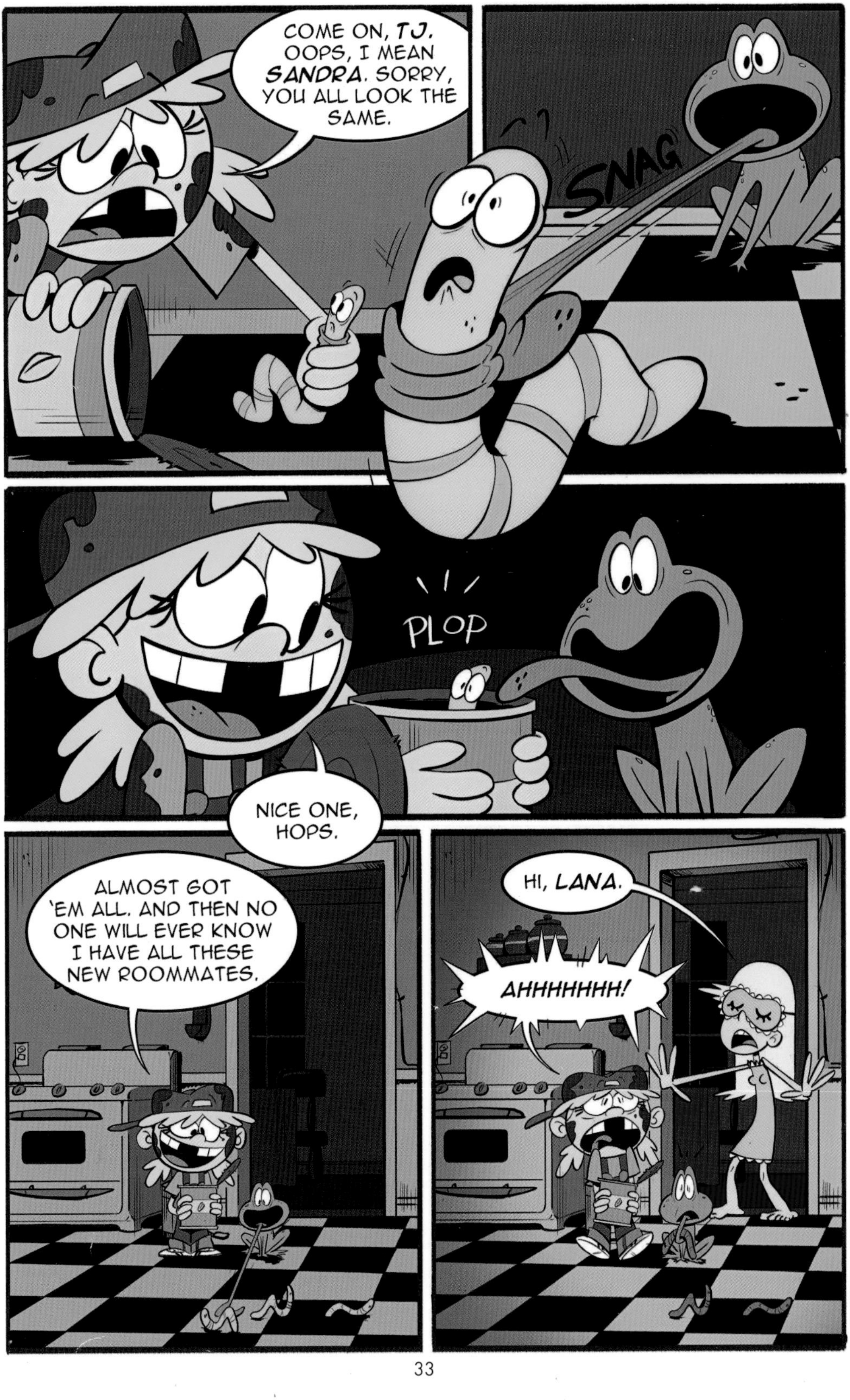
COME ON, TJ. OOPS, I MEAN SANDRA. SORRY, YOU ALL LOOK THE SAME.
SNAG
PLOP
NICE ONE, HOPS.
ALMOST GOT 'EM ALL. AND THEN NO ONE WILL EVER KNOW I HAVE ALL THESE NEW ROOMMATES.
HI, LANA.
AHHHHHHH!

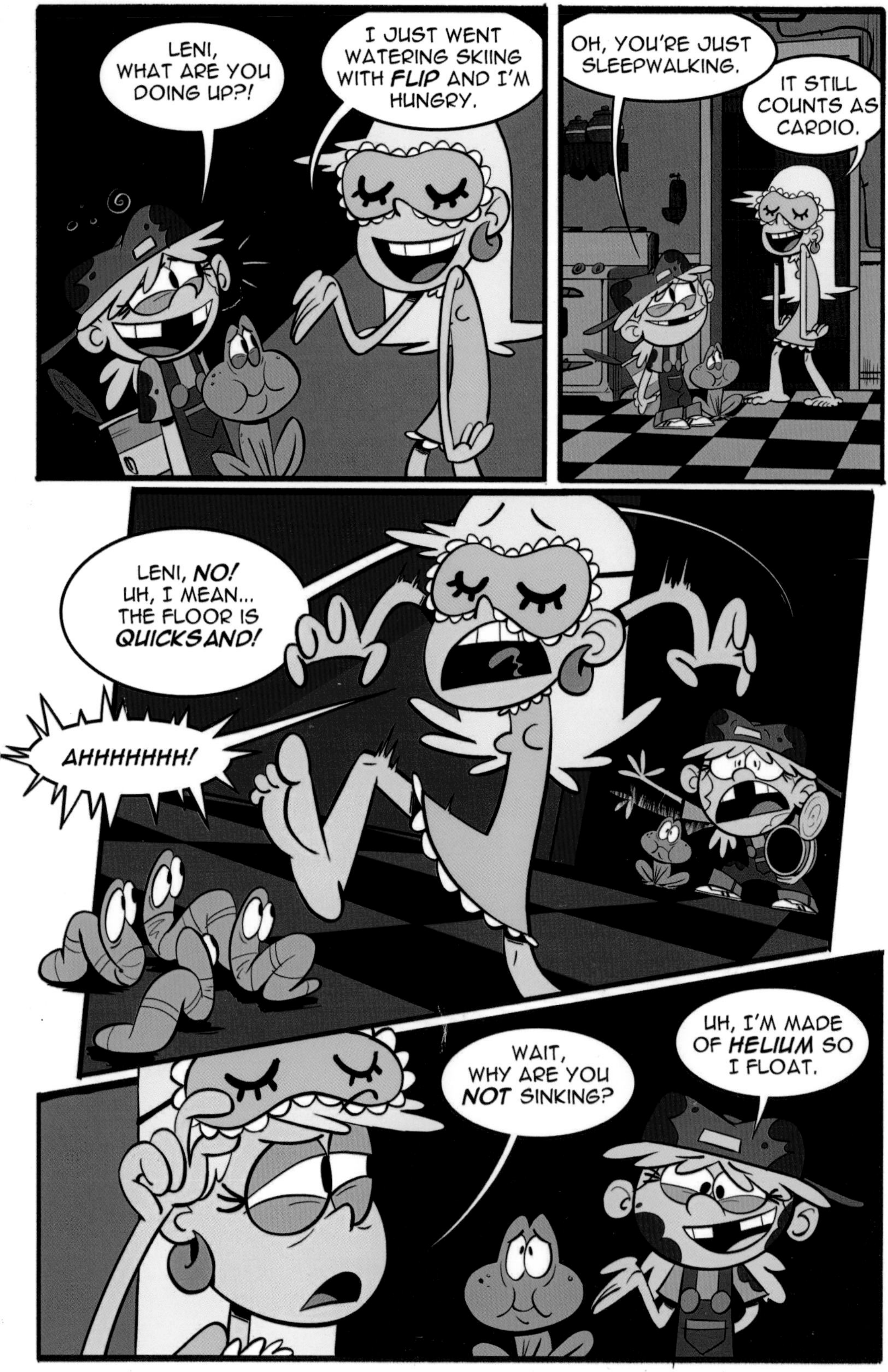
LENI, WHAT ARE YOU DOING UP?!
I JUST WENT WATERING SKIING WITH FLIP AND I'M HUNGRY.
OH, YOU'RE JUST SLEEPWALKING.
IT STILL COUNTS AS CARDIO.
LENI, NO! UH, I MEAN... THE FLOOR IS QUICKSAND!
AHHHHHHH!
WAIT, WHY ARE YOU NOT SINKING?
UH, I'M MADE OF HELIUM SO I FLOAT.

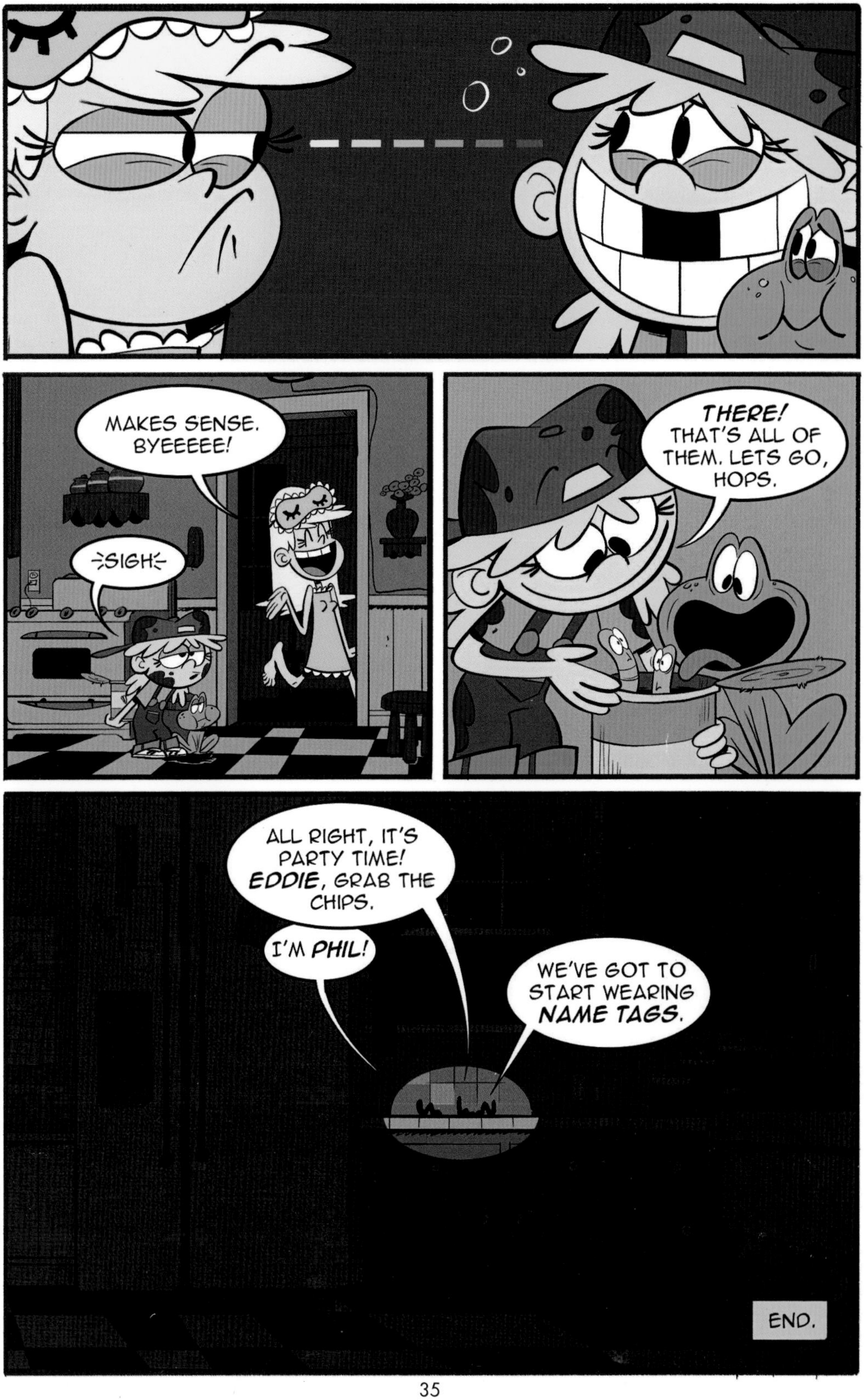
MAKES SENSE. BYEEEEE!
SIGH
THERE! THAT'S ALL OF THEM. LETS GO, HOPS.
ALL RIGHT, IT'S PARTY TIME! EDDIE, GRAB THE CHIPS.
I'M PHIL!
WE'VE GOT TO START WEARING NAME TAGS.
END.

"3:00 AM: SHIPS IN THE NIGHT"

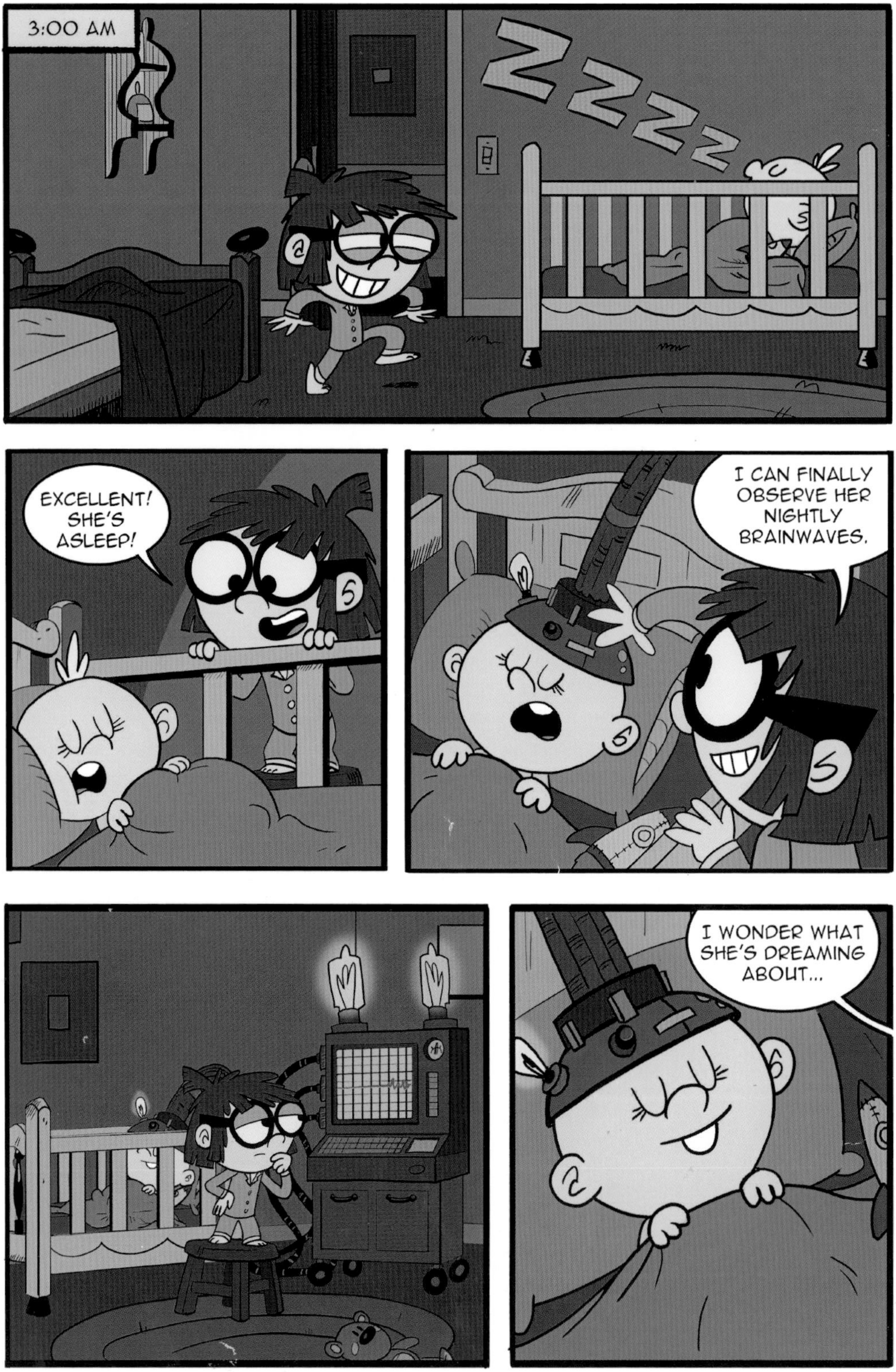
3:00 AM
ZZZZZ
EXCELLENT! SHE'S ASLEEP!
I CAN FINALLY OBSERVE HER NIGHTLY BRAINWAVES.
I WONDER WHAT SHE'S DREAMING ABOUT...

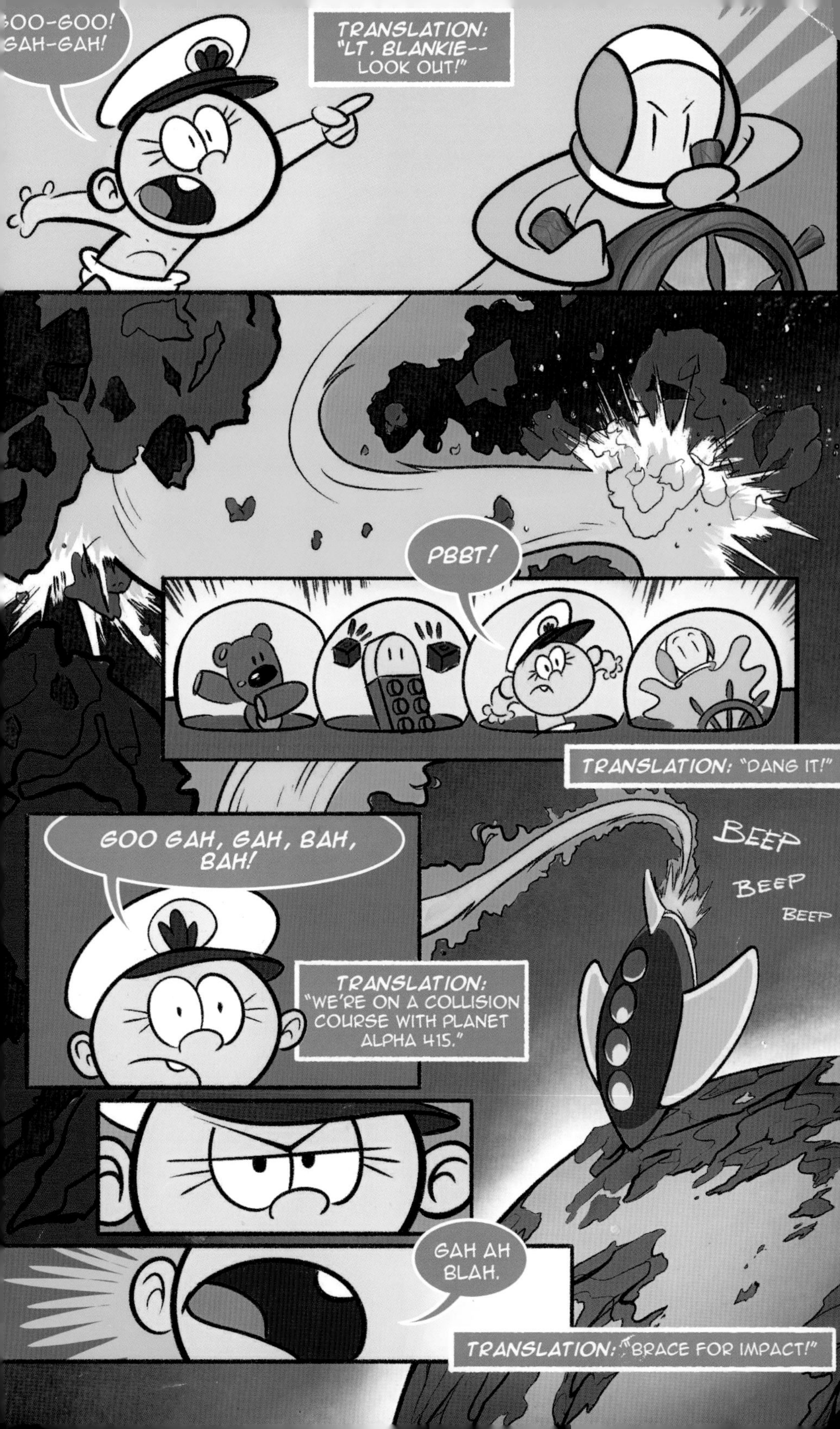
GOO-GOO! GAH-GAH!
TRANSLATION: "LT. BLANKIE-- LOOK OUT!"
PBBT!
TRANSLATION: "DANG IT!"
GOO GAH, GAH, BAH, BAH!
TRANSLATION: "WE'RE ON A COLLISION COURSE WITH PLANET ALPHA 415."
BEEP
BEEP
BEEP
GAH AH BLAH.
TRANSLATION: "BRACE FOR IMPACT!"

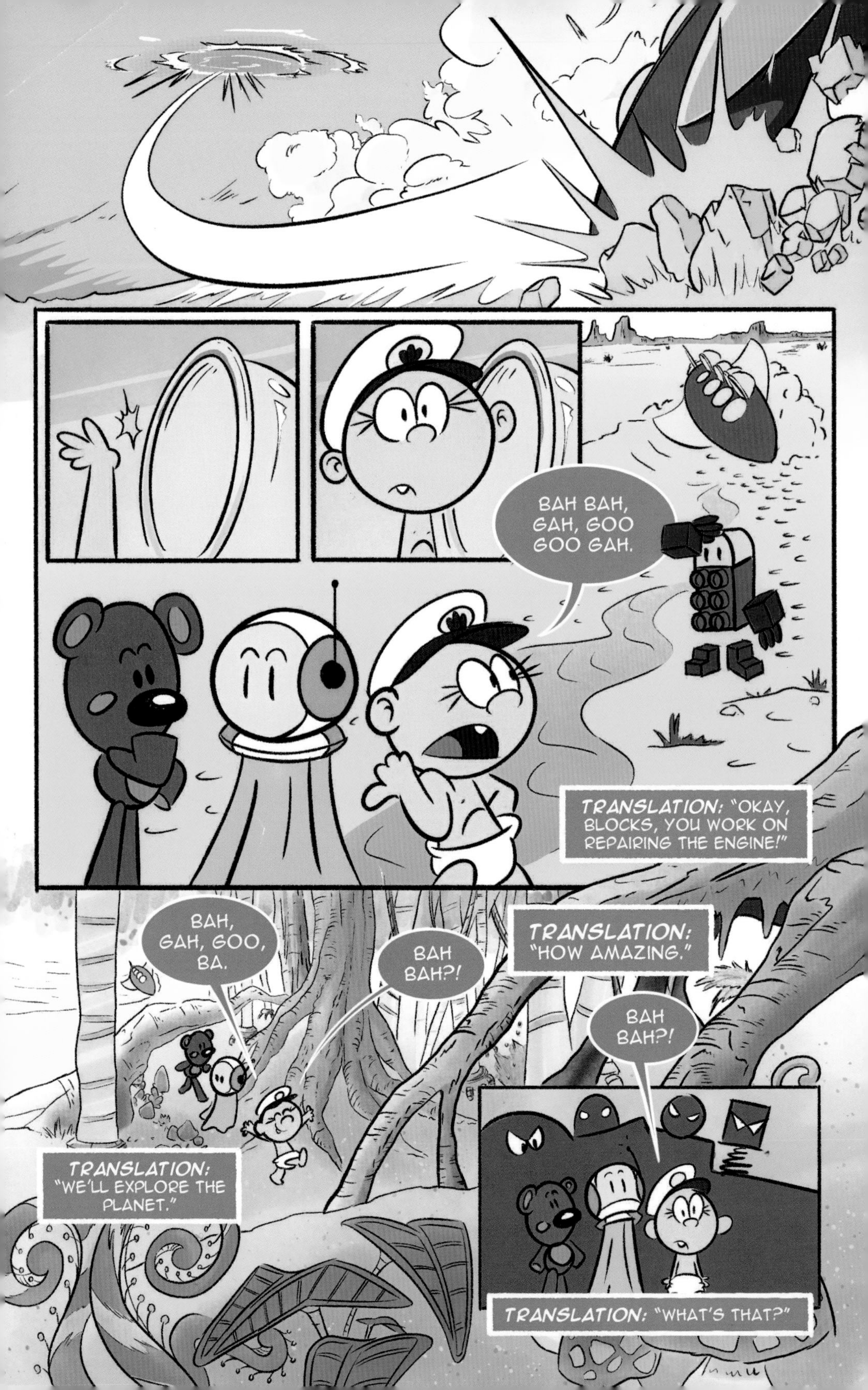
BAH BAH, GAH, GOO GOO GAH.
TRANSLATION: "OKAY, BLOCKS, YOU WORK ON REPAIRING THE ENGINE!"
BAH, GAH, GOO, BA.
TRANSLATION: "WE'LL EXPLORE THE PLANET."
BAH BAH?!
TRANSLATION: "HOW AMAZING."
BAH BAH?!
TRANSLATION: "WHAT'S THAT?"

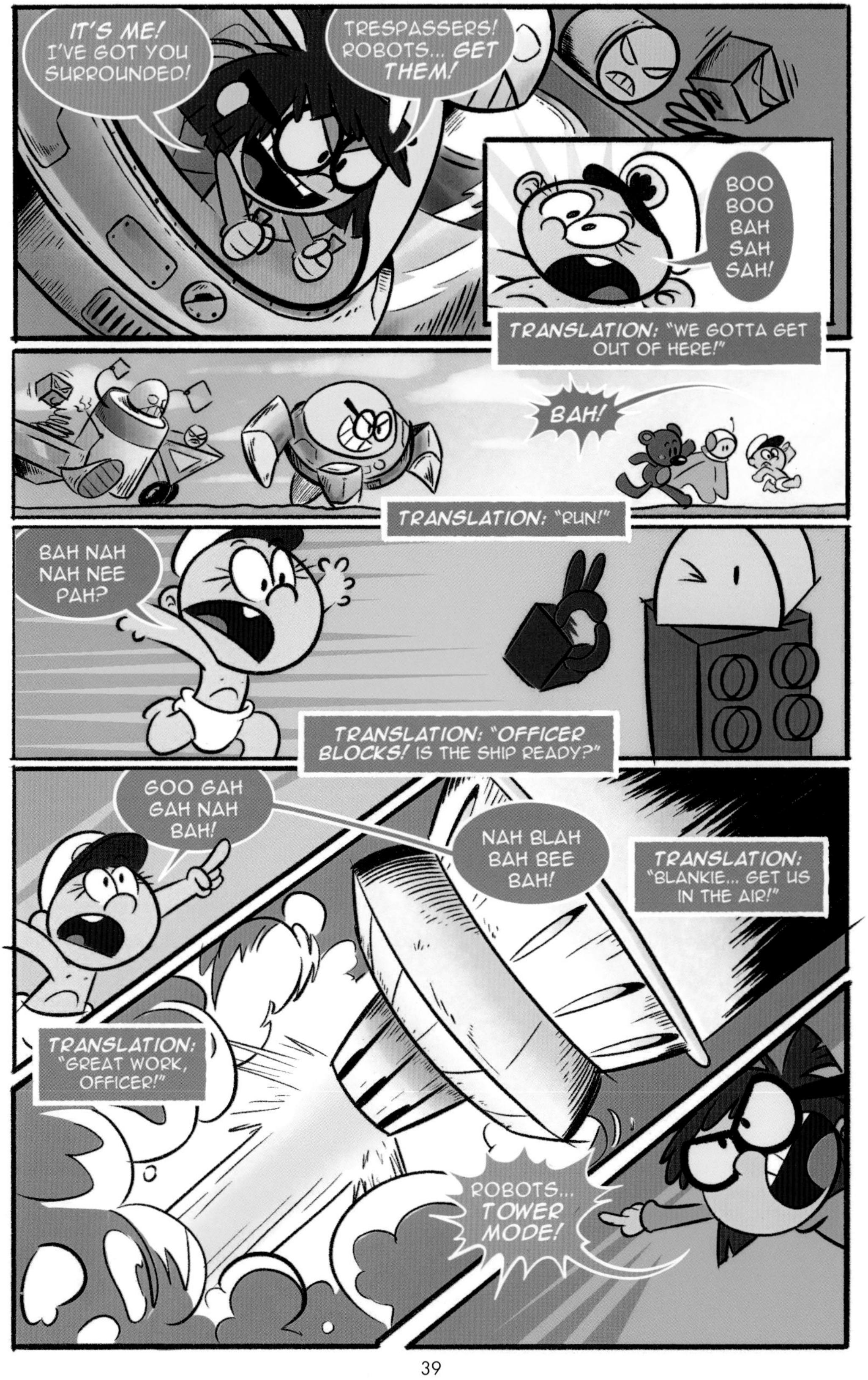

IT'S ME! I'VE GOT YOU SURROUNDED!
TRESPASSERS! ROBOTS... GET THEM!
BOO BOO BAH SAH SAH!
TRANSLATION: "WE GOTTA GET OUT OF HERE!"
BAH!
TRANSLATION: "RUN!"
BAH NAH NAH NEE PAH?
TRANSLATION: "OFFICER BLOCKS! IS THE SHIP READY?"
GOO GAH GAH NAH BAH!
NAH BLAH BAH BEE BAH!
TRANSLATION: "BLANKIE... GET US IN THE AIR!"
TRANSLATION: "GREAT WORK, OFFICER!"
ROBOTS... TOWER MODE!

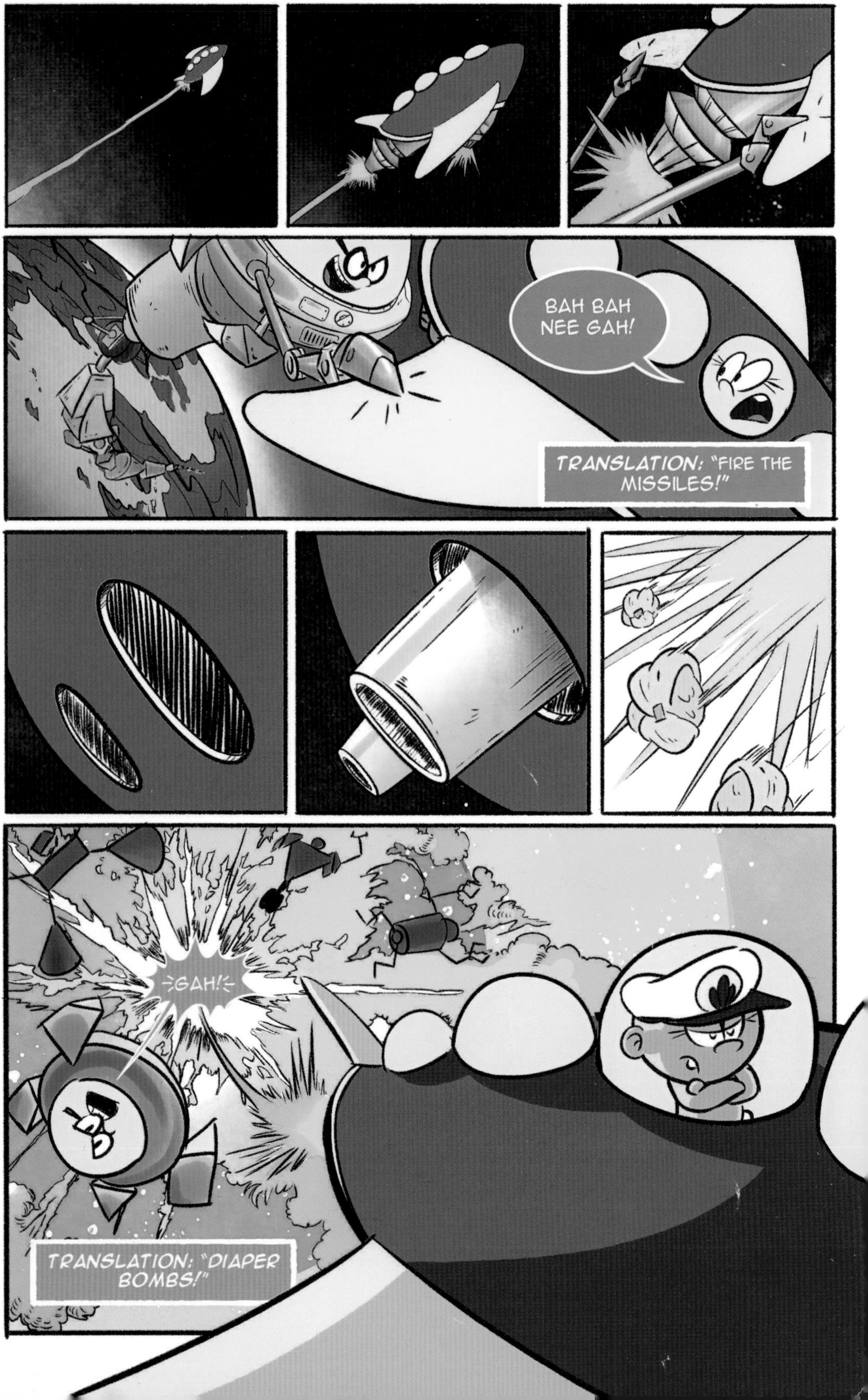
BAH BAH NEE GAH!
TRANSLATION: "FIRE THE MISSILES!"
GAH!
TRANSLATION: "DIAPER BOMBS!"

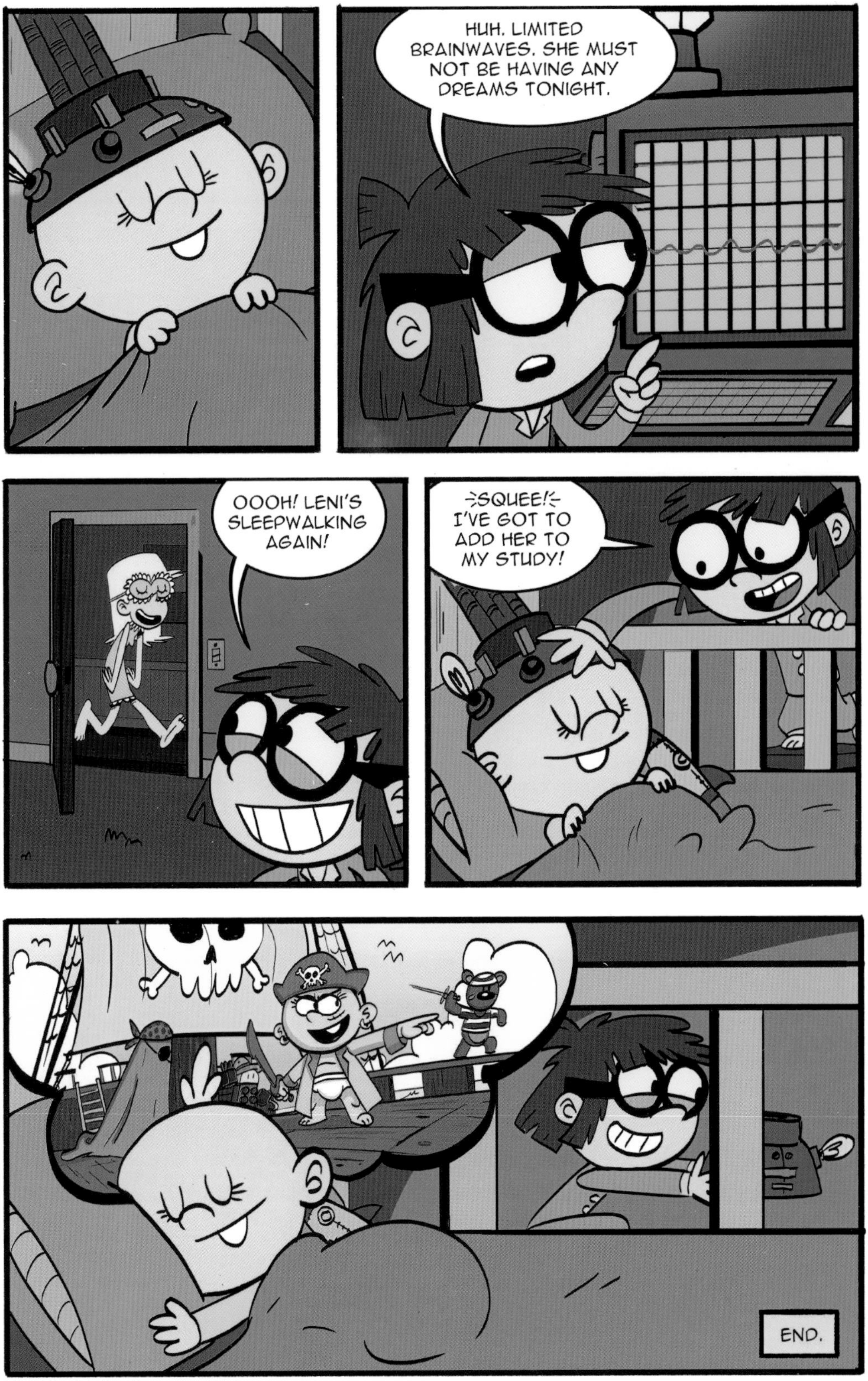
HUH. LIMITED BRAINWAVES. SHE MUST NOT BE HAVING ANY DREAMS TONIGHT.
OOOH! LENI'S SLEEPWALKING AGAIN!
SQUEE! I'VE GOT TO ADD HER TO MY STUDY!
END.

"3:55 AM: BUSTED"

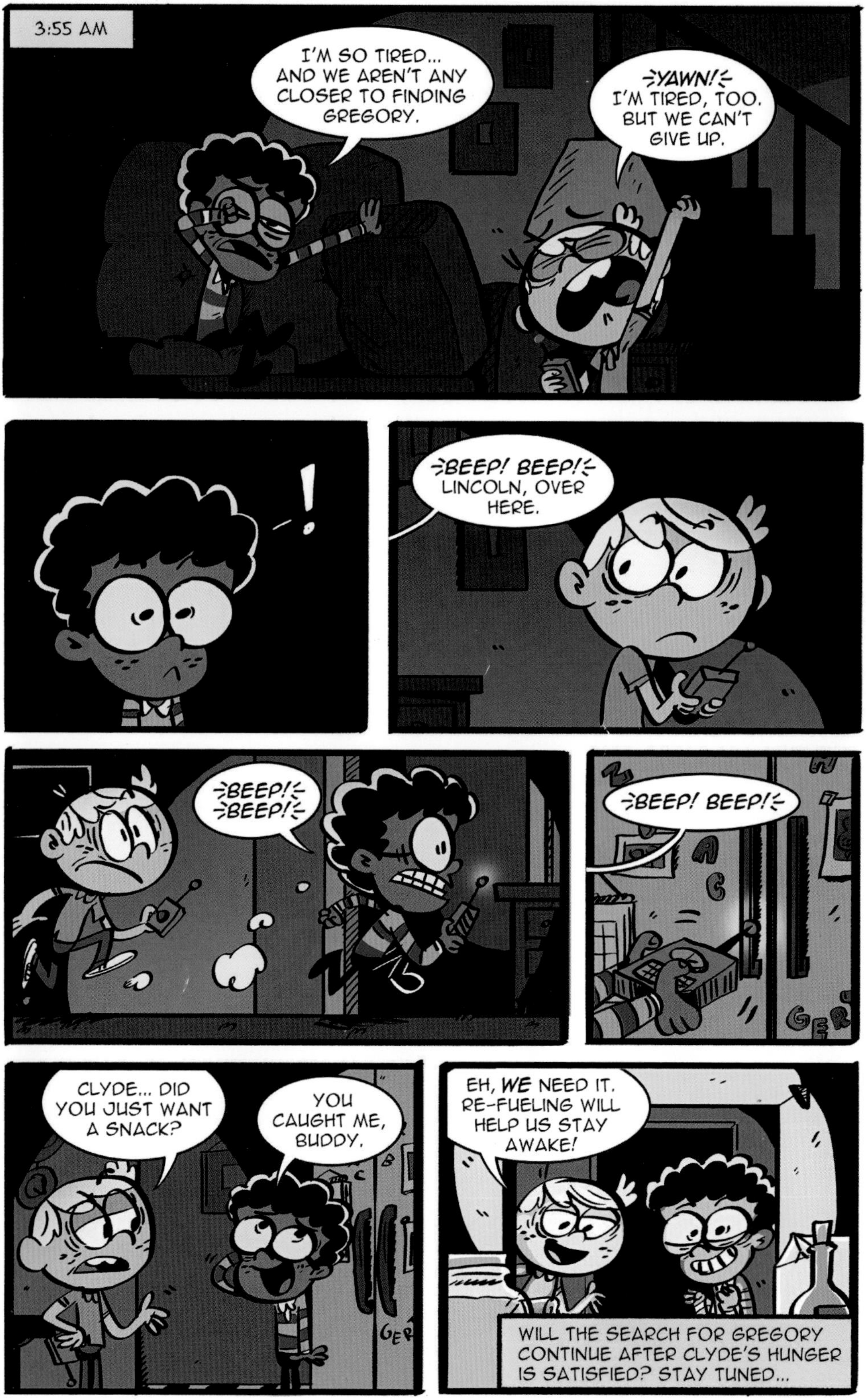
3:55 AM
I'M SO TIRED... AND WE AREN'T ANY CLOSER TO FINDING GREGORY.
YAWN! I'M TIRED, TOO. BUT WE CAN'T GIVE UP.
!
BEEP! BEEP! LINCOLN, OVER HERE.
BEEP! BEEP!
BEEP! BEEP!
CLYDE... DID YOU JUST WANT A SNACK?
YOU CAUGHT ME, BUDDY.
EH, WE NEED IT. RE-FUELING WILL HELP US STAY AWAKE!
WILL THE SEARCH FOR GREGORY CONTINUE AFTER CLYDE'S HUNGER IS SATISFIED? STAY TUNED...

"4:00 AM: THE PRINCESS AND THE PLEA"

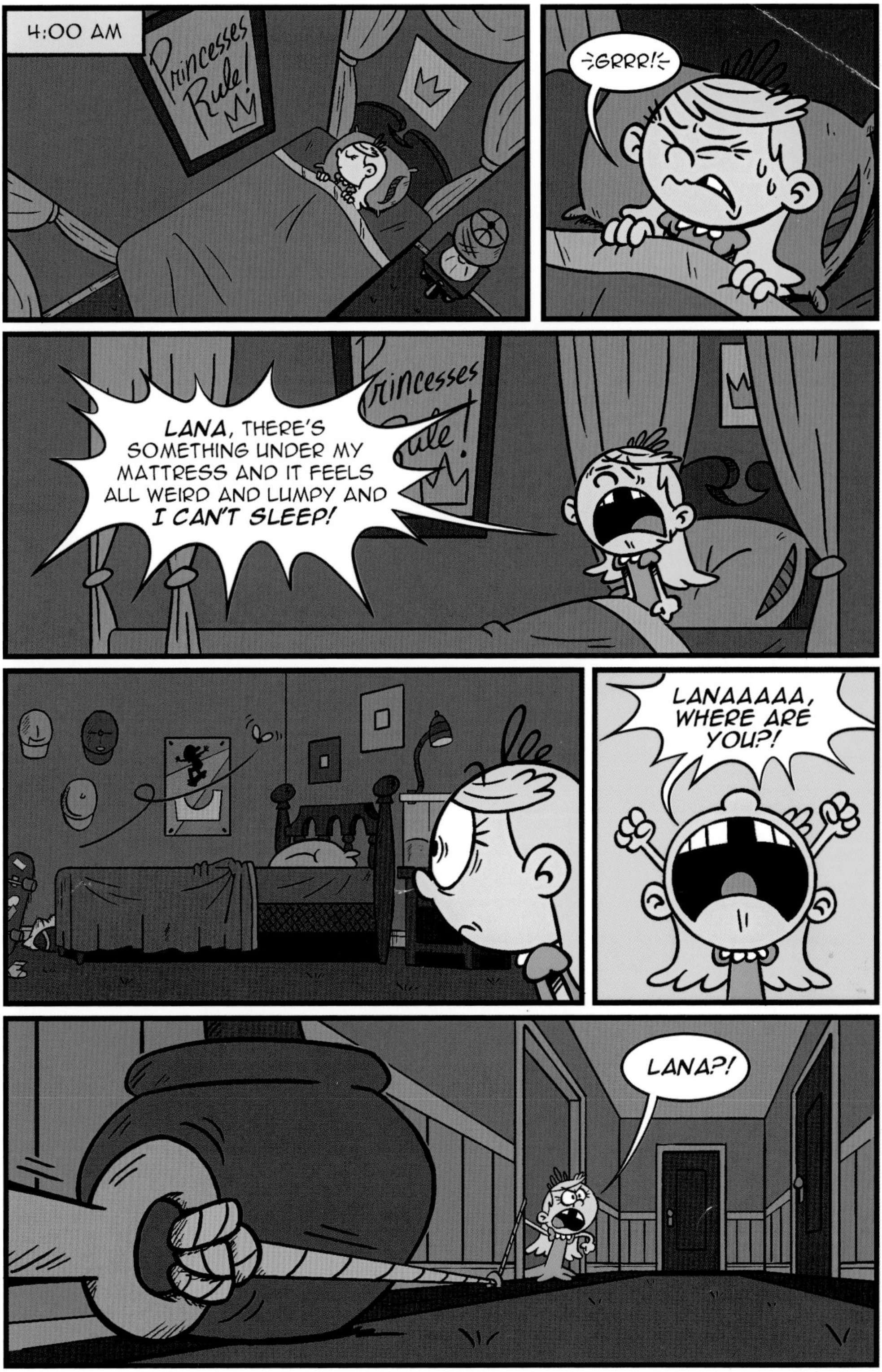
4:00 AM
Princesses Rule!
GRRR!
LANA, THERE'S SOMETHING UNDER MY MATTRESS AND IT FEELS ALL WEIRD AND LUMPY AND I CAN'T SLEEP!
LANAAAAA, WHERE ARE YOU?!
LANA?!

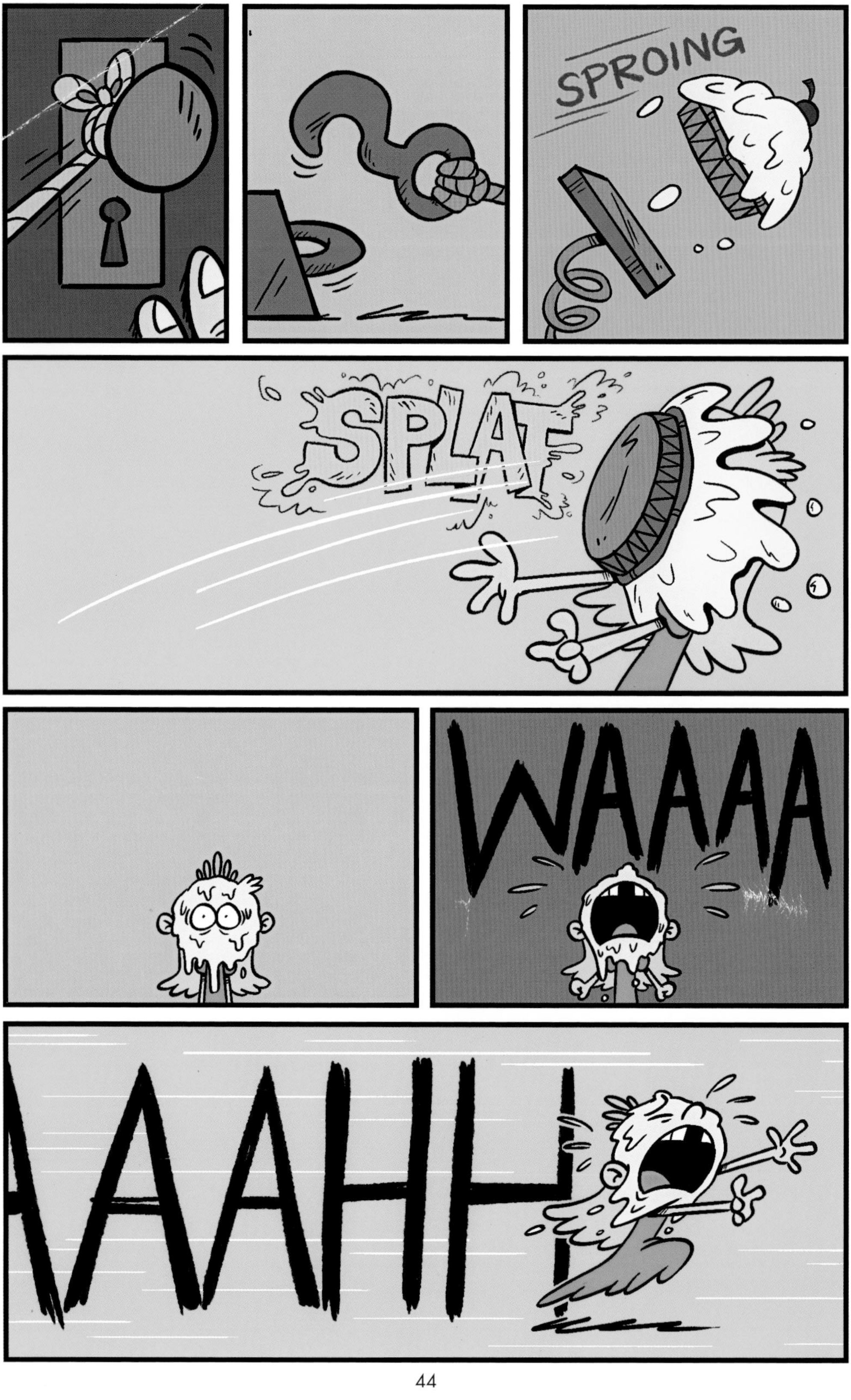
SPROING
SPLAT
WAAAA
AAHH!

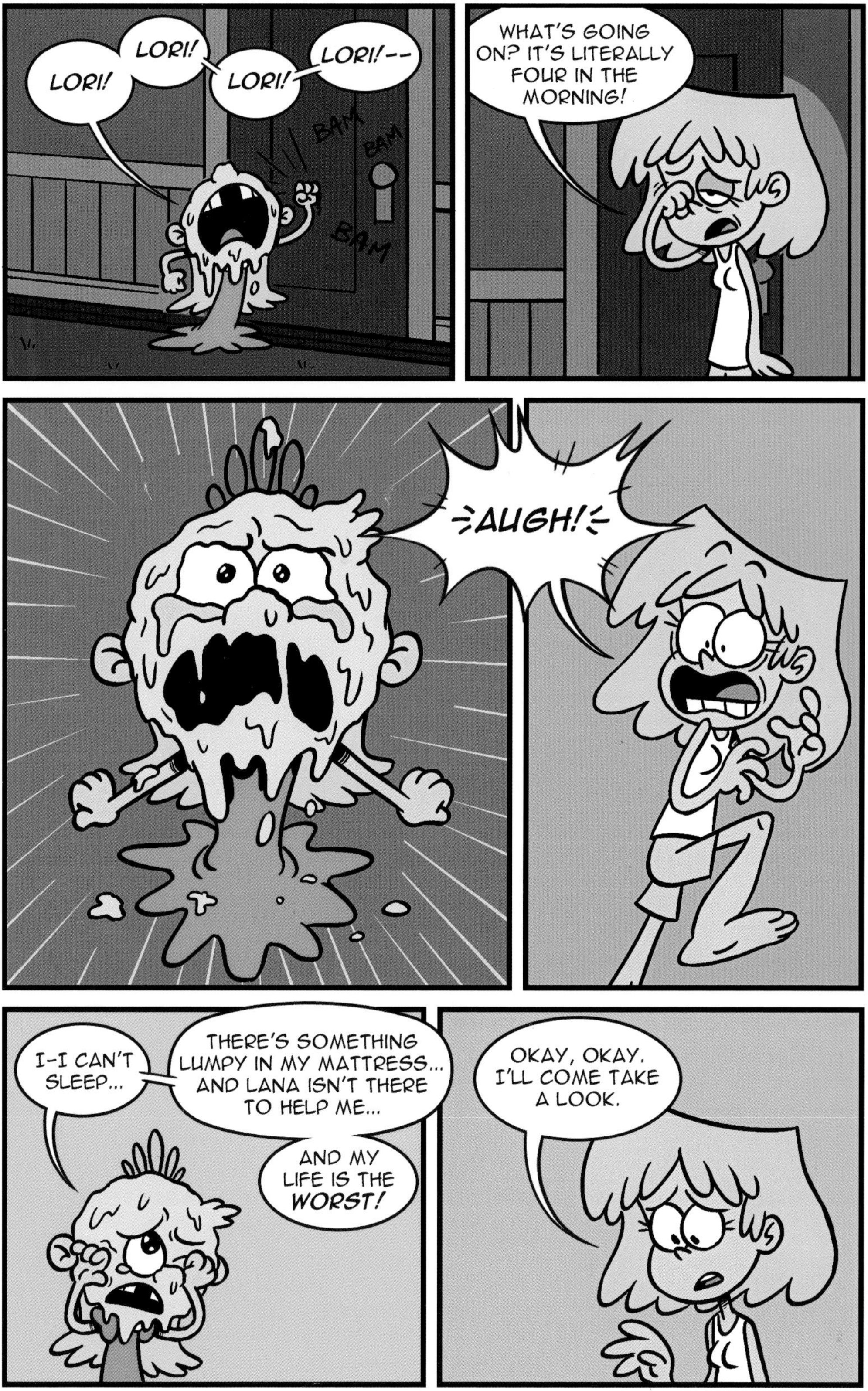
LORI!
LORI!
LORI!
LORI!--
BAM
BAM
BAM
WHAT'S GOING ON? IT'S LITERALLY FOUR IN THE MORNING!
AUGH!
I-I CAN'T SLEEP...
THERE'S SOMETHING LUMPY IN MY MATTRESS... AND LANA ISN'T THERE TO HELP ME...
AND MY LIFE IS THE WORST!
OKAY, OKAY. I'LL COME TAKE A LOOK.

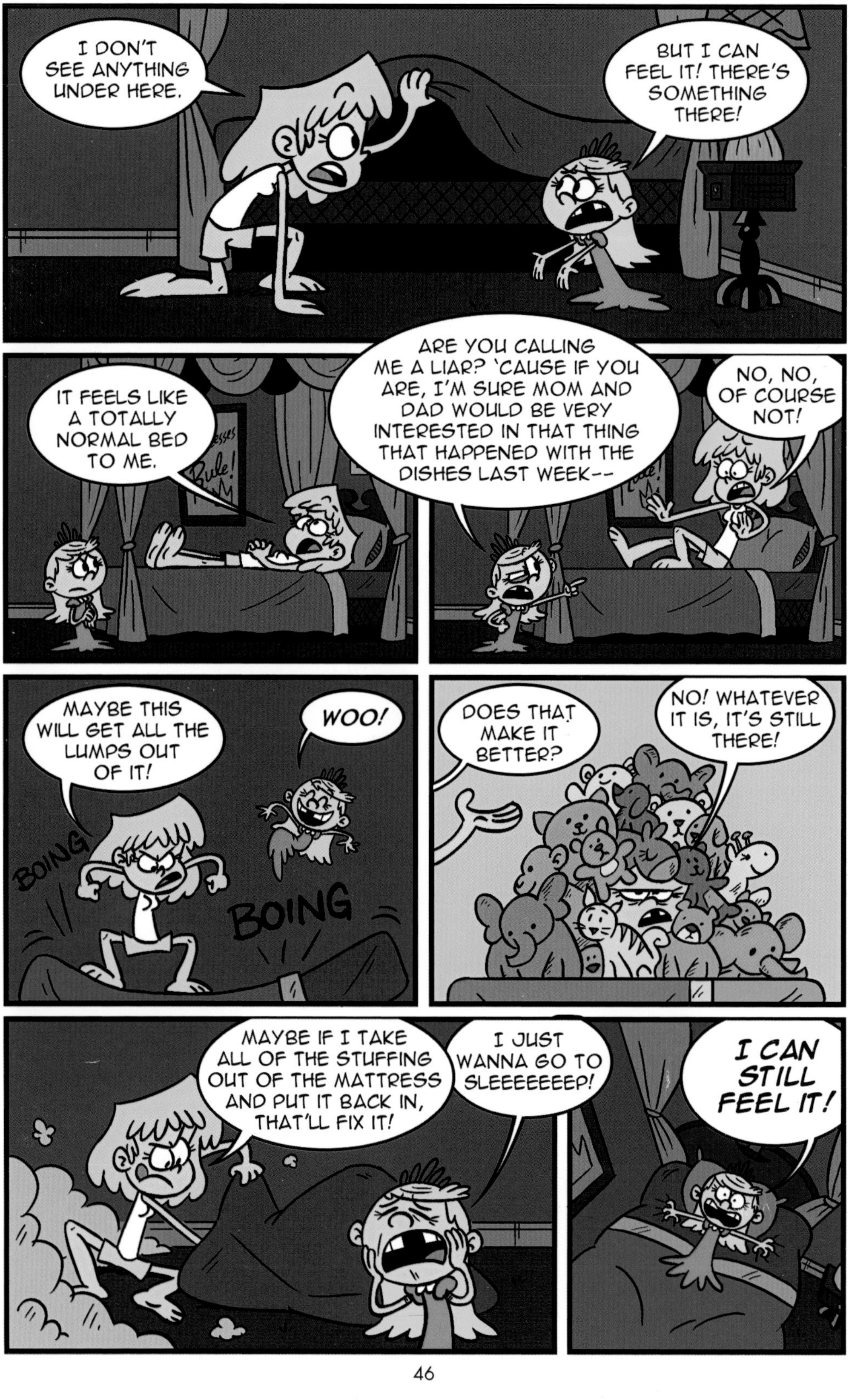
I DON'T SEE ANYTHING UNDER HERE.
BUT I CAN FEEL IT! THERE'S SOMETHING THERE!
IT FEELS LIKE A TOTALLY NORMAL BED TO ME.
ARE YOU CALLING ME A LIAR? 'CAUSE IF YOU ARE, I'M SURE MOM AND DAD WOULD BE VERY INTERESTED IN THAT THING THAT HAPPENED WITH THE DISHES LAST WEEK--
NO, NO, OF COURSE NOT!
MAYBE THIS WILL GET ALL THE LUMPS OUT OF IT!
WOO!
BOING
BOING
DOES THAT MAKE IT BETTER?
NO! WHATEVER IT IS, IT'S STILL THERE!
MAYBE IF I TAKE ALL OF THE STUFFING OUT OF THE MATTRESS AND PUT IT BACK IN, THAT'LL FIX IT!
I JUST WANNA GO TO SLEEEEEEEP!
I CAN STILL FEEL IT!

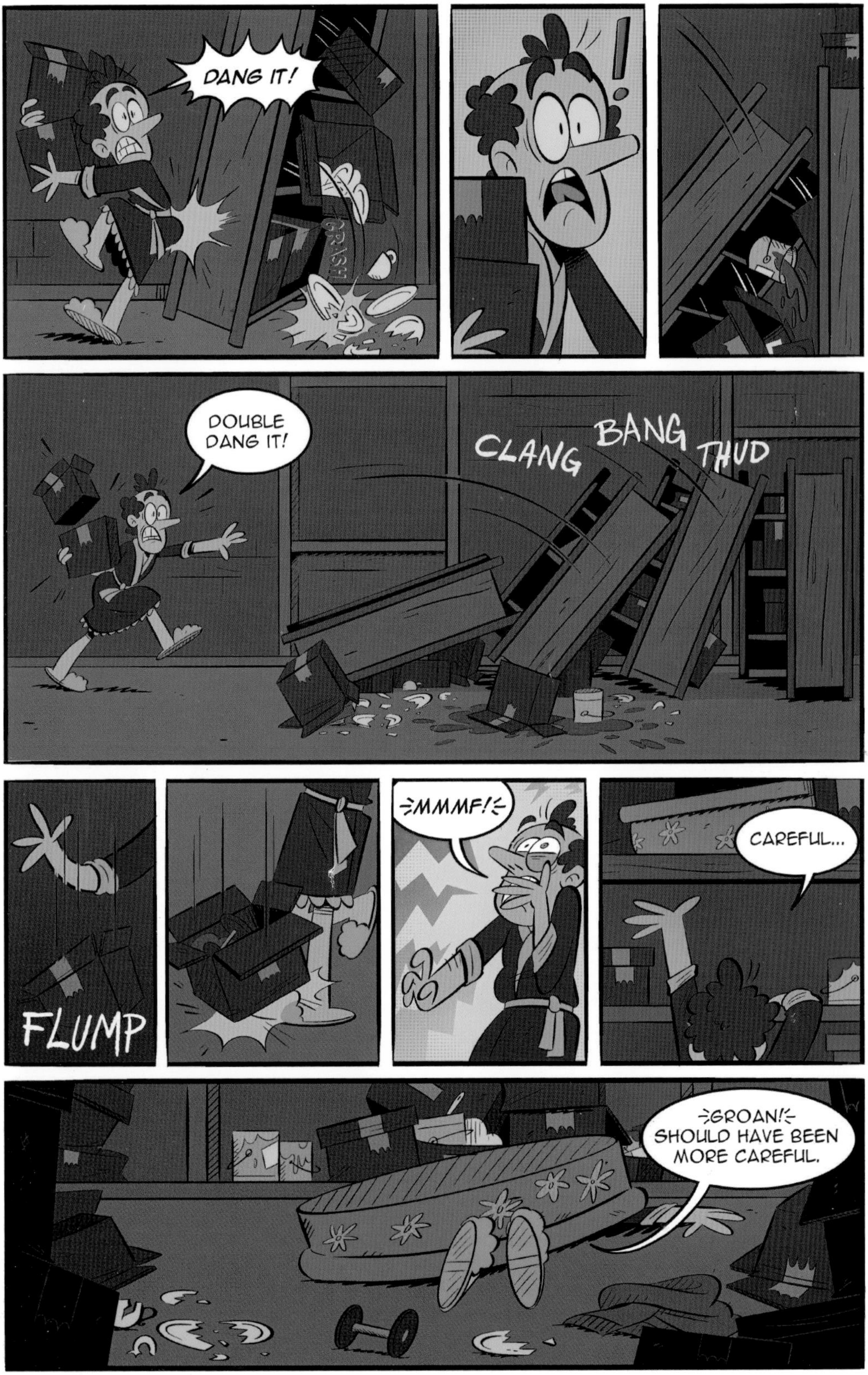
DANG IT!
CRASH
!
DOUBLE DANG IT!
CLANG
BANG
THUD
FLUMP
MMMF!
CAREFUL...
GROAN!
SHOULD HAVE BEEN MORE CAREFUL.

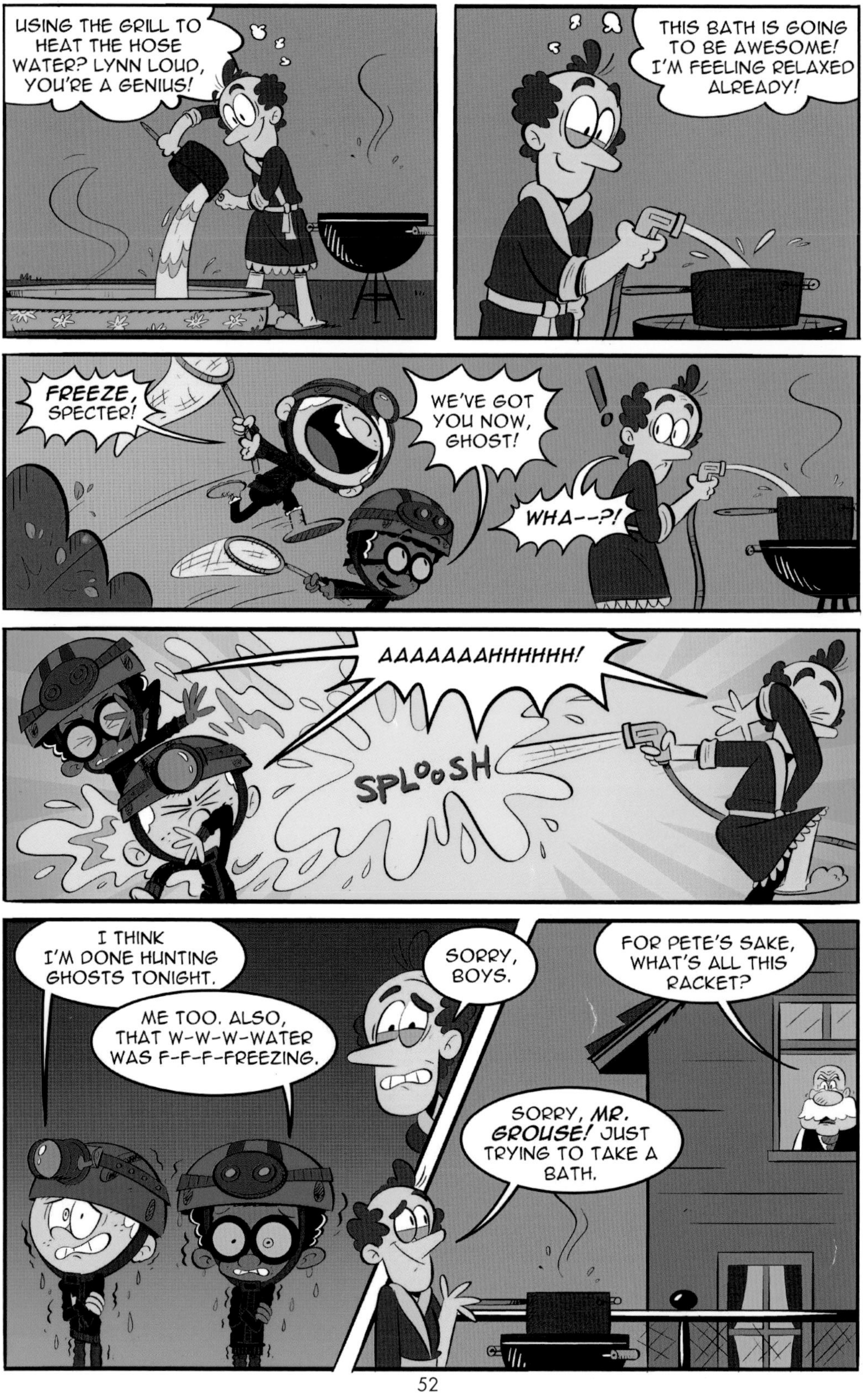
USING THE GRILL TO HEAT THE HOSE WATER? LYNN LOUD, YOU'RE A GENIUS!
THIS BATH IS GOING TO BE AWESOME! I'M FEELING RELAXED ALREADY!
FREEZE, SPECTER!
WE'VE GOT YOU NOW, GHOST!
!
WHA--?!
AAAAAAAHHHHHH!
SPLOOSH
I THINK I'M DONE HUNTING GHOSTS TONIGHT.
ME TOO. ALSO, THAT W-W-W-WATER WAS F-F-F-FREEZING.
SORRY, BOYS.
FOR PETE'S SAKE, WHAT'S ALL THIS RACKET?
SORRY, MR. GROUSE! JUST TRYING TO TAKE A BATH.

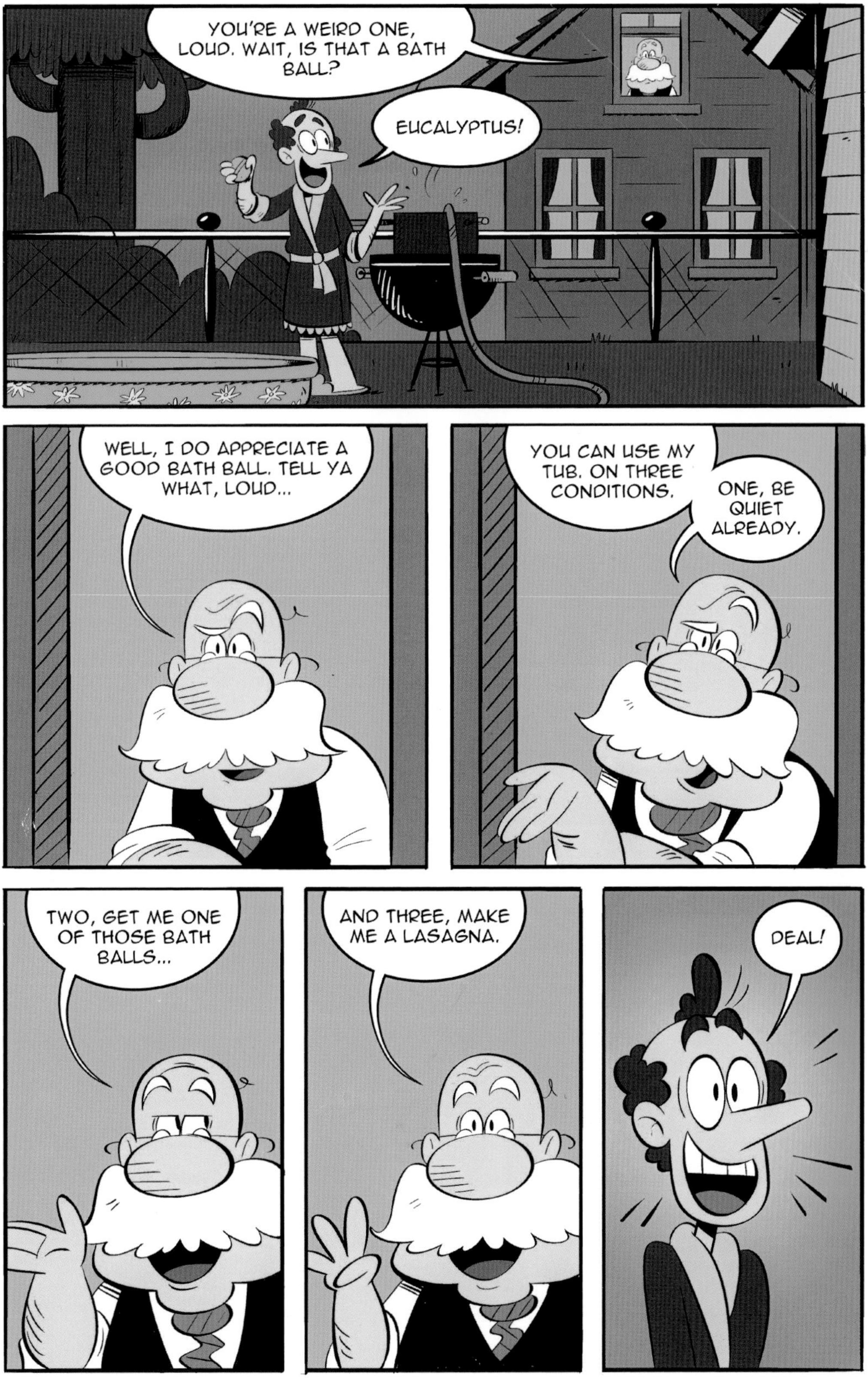
YOU'RE A WEIRD ONE, LOUD. WAIT, IS THAT A BATH BALL?
EUCALYPTUS!
WELL, I DO APPRECIATE A GOOD BATH BALL. TELL YA WHAT, LOUD...
YOU CAN USE MY TUB. ON THREE CONDITIONS.
ONE, BE QUIET ALREADY.
TWO, GET ME ONE OF THOSE BATH BALLS...
AND THREE, MAKE ME A LASAGNA.
DEAL!

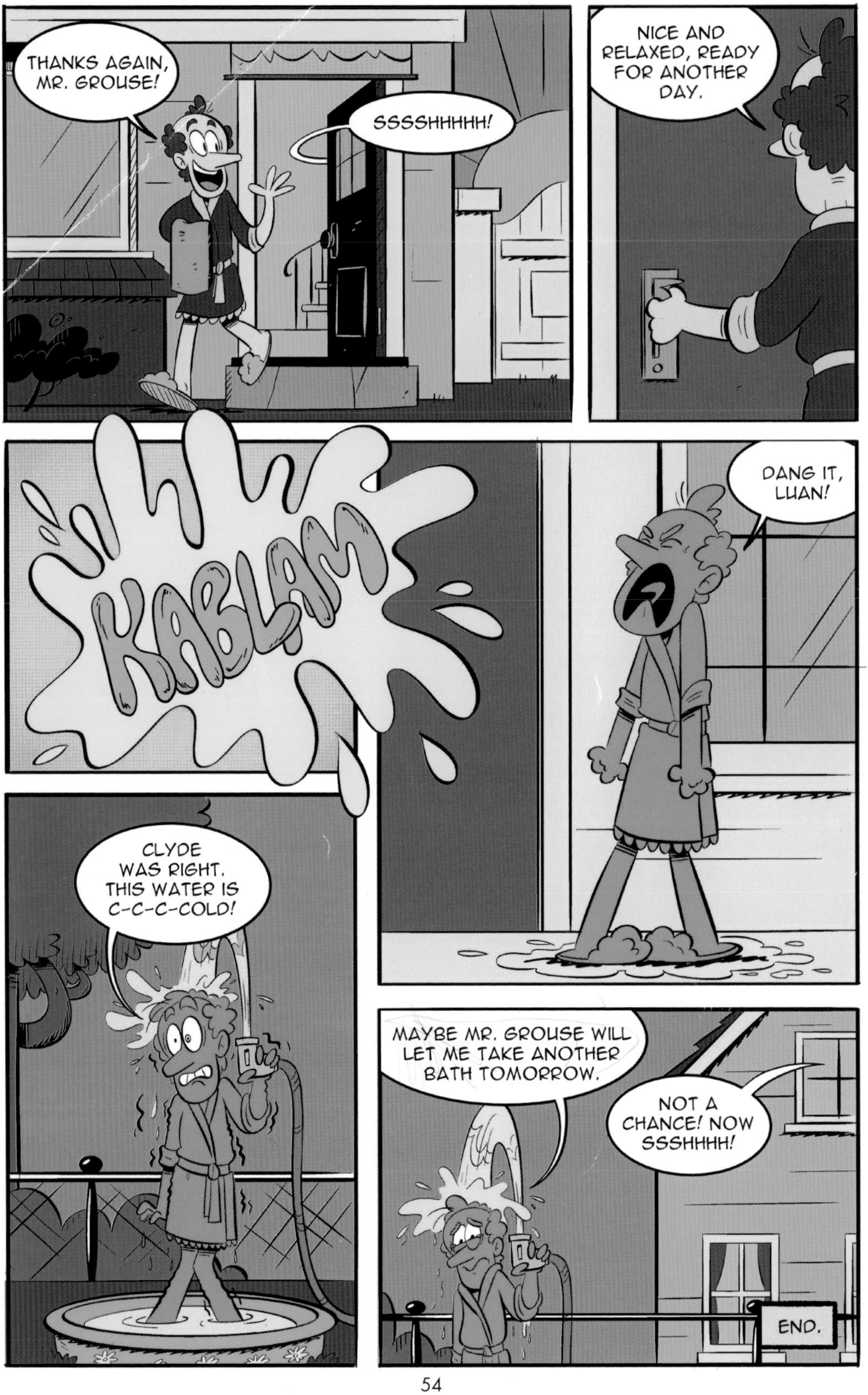
THANKS AGAIN, MR. GROUSE!
SSSSHHHHH!
NICE AND RELAXED, READY FOR ANOTHER DAY.
KABLAM
DANG IT, LUAN!
CLYDE WAS RIGHT. THIS WATER IS C-C-C-COLD!
MAYBE MR. GROUSE WILL LET ME TAKE ANOTHER BATH TOMORROW.
NOT A CHANCE! NOW SSSHHHH!
END.

5:55 AM BOYS IN THE ATTIC

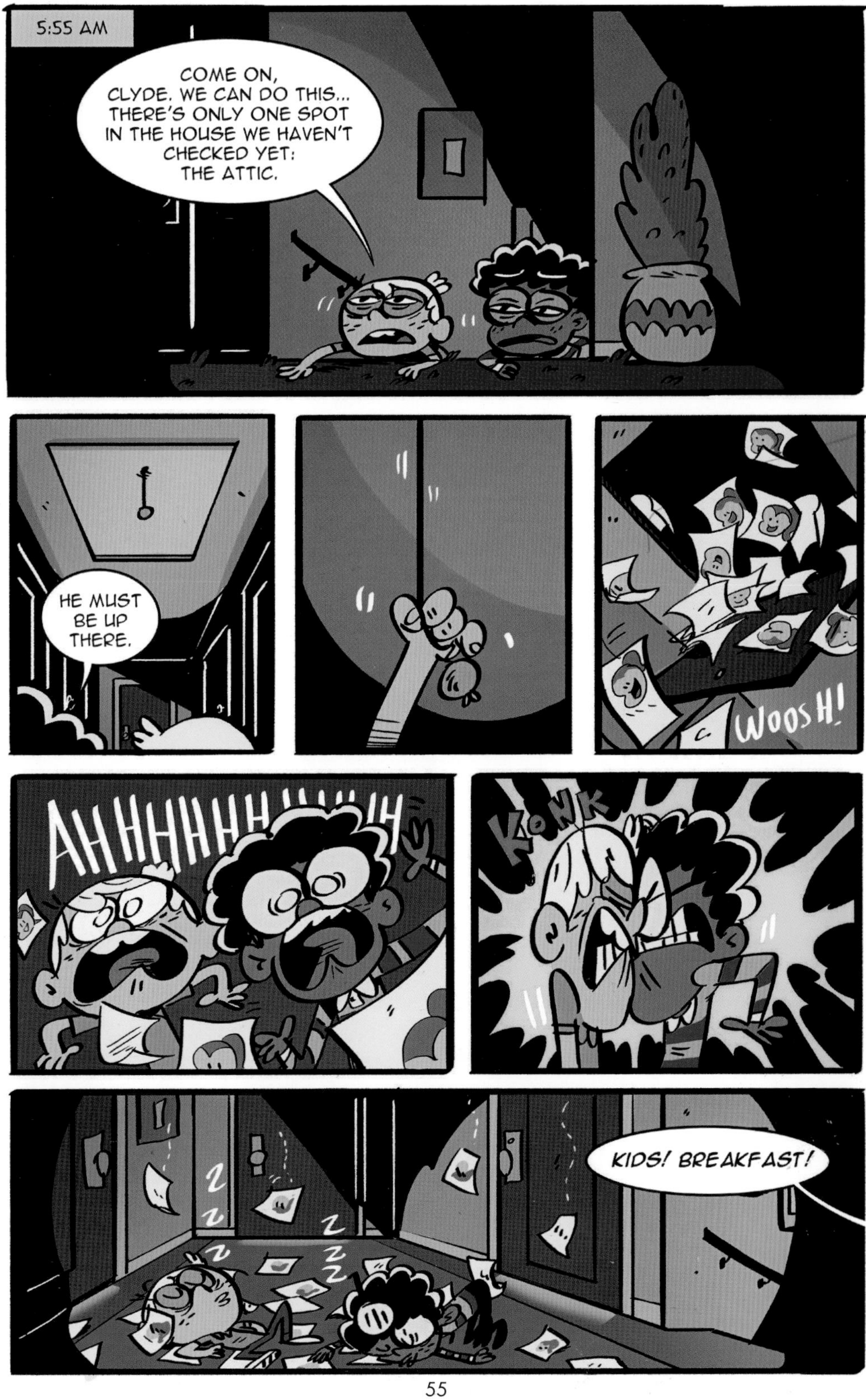
5:55 AM
COME ON, CLYDE. WE CAN DO THIS... THERE'S ONLY ONE SPOT IN THE HOUSE WE HAVEN'T CHECKED YET: THE ATTIC.
HE MUST BE UP THERE.
WOOSH!
KONK
KIDS! BREAKFAST!

"6:00 AM: BREAKFAST IS READY!"

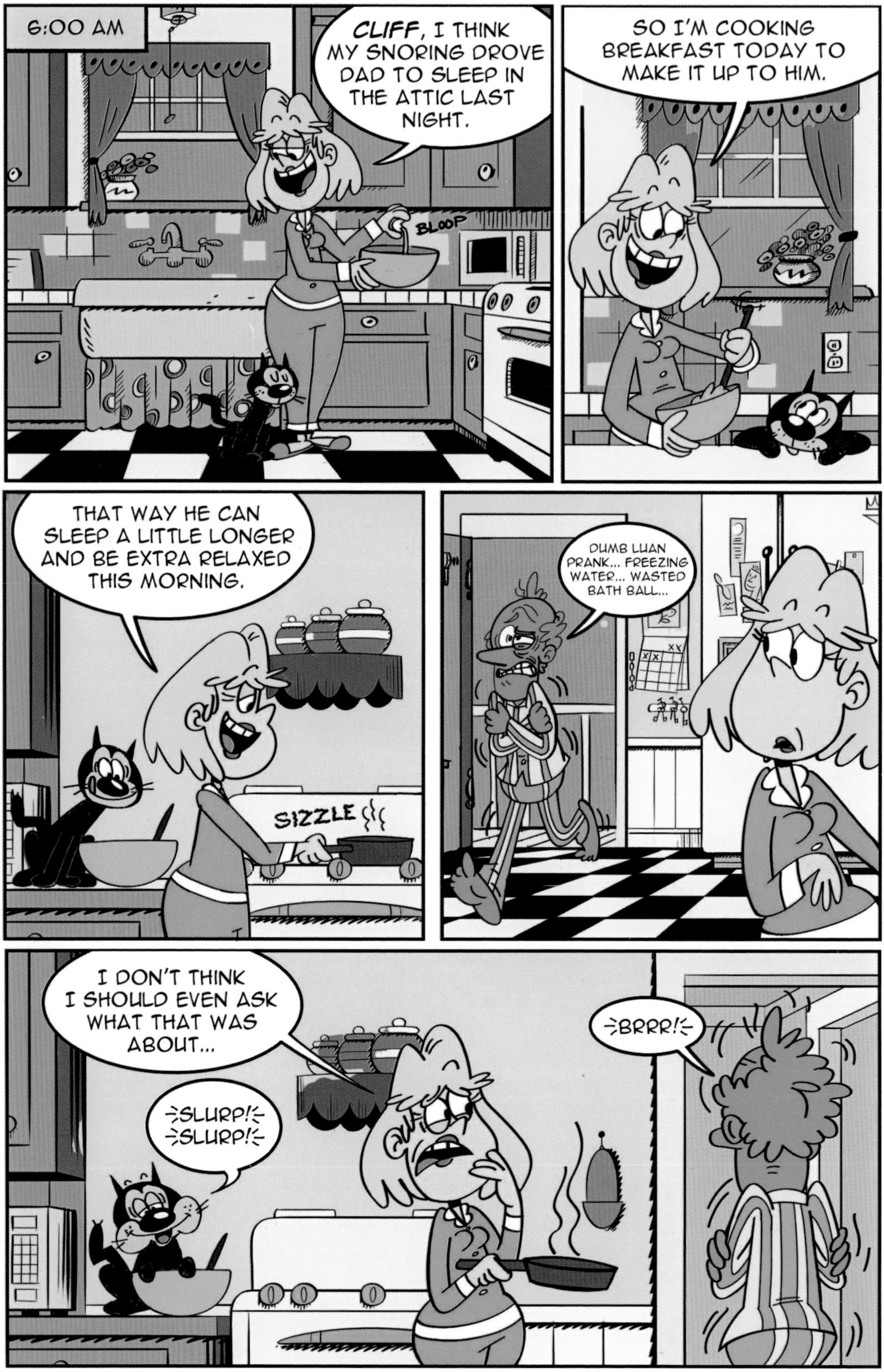

6:00 AM
CLIFF, I THINK MY SNORING DROVE DAD TO SLEEP IN THE ATTIC LAST NIGHT.
BLOOP
SO I'M COOKING BREAKFAST TODAY TO MAKE IT UP TO HIM.
THAT WAY HE CAN SLEEP A LITTLE LONGER AND BE EXTRA RELAXED THIS MORNING.
SIZZLE
DUMB LUAN PRANK... FREEZING WATER... WASTED BATH BALL...
I DON'T THINK I SHOULD EVEN ASK WHAT THAT WAS ABOUT...
SLURP! SLURP!
BRRR!

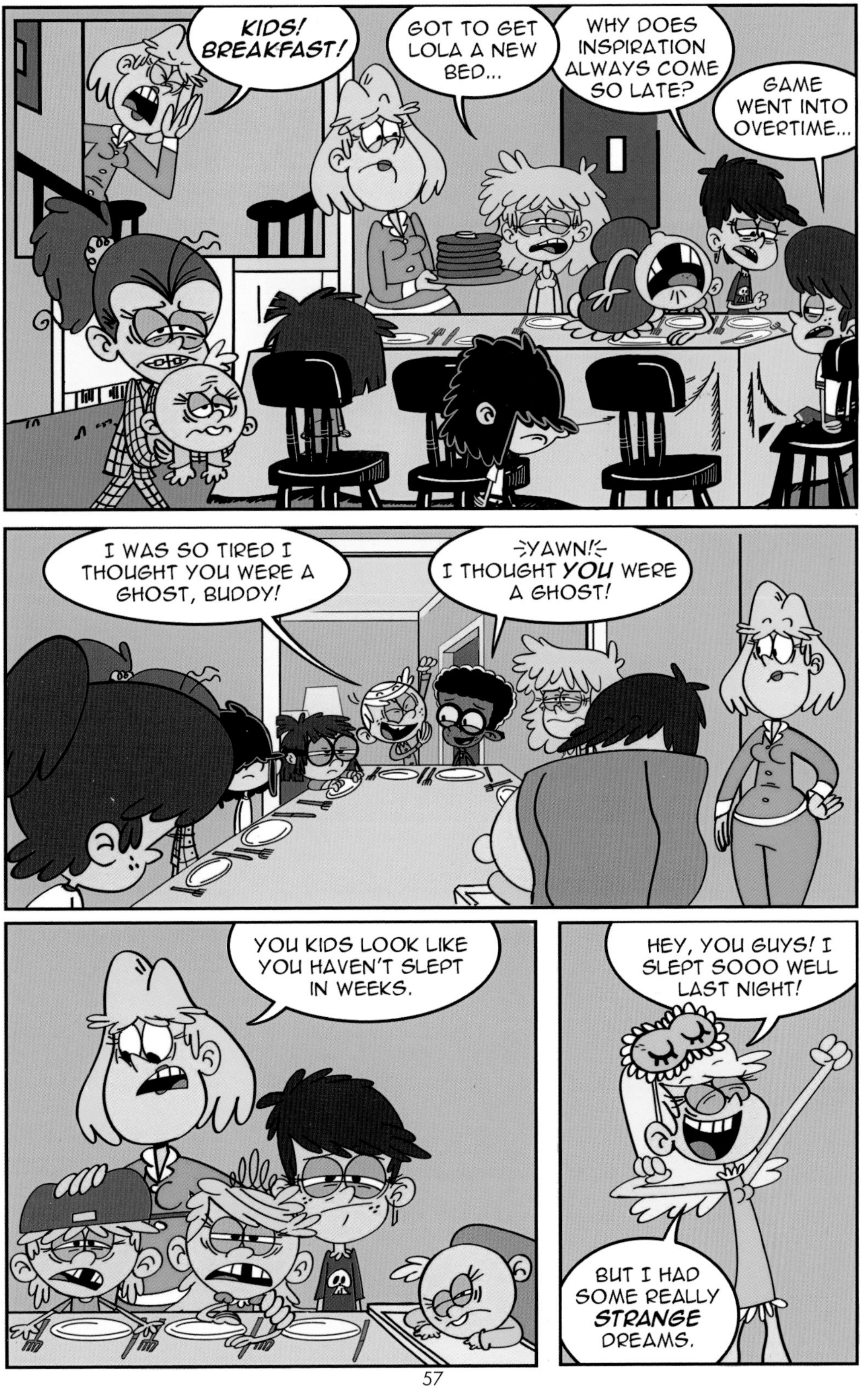
KIDS! BREAKFAST!
GOT TO GET LOLA A NEW BED...
WHY DOES INSPIRATION ALWAYS COME SO LATE?
GAME WENT INTO OVERTIME...
I WAS SO TIRED I THOUGHT YOU WERE A GHOST, BUDDY!
YAWN! I THOUGHT YOU WERE A GHOST!
YOU KIDS LOOK LIKE YOU HAVEN'T SLEPT IN WEEKS.
HEY, YOU GUYS! I SLEPT SOOO WELL LAST NIGHT!
BUT I HAD SOME REALLY STRANGE DREAMS.

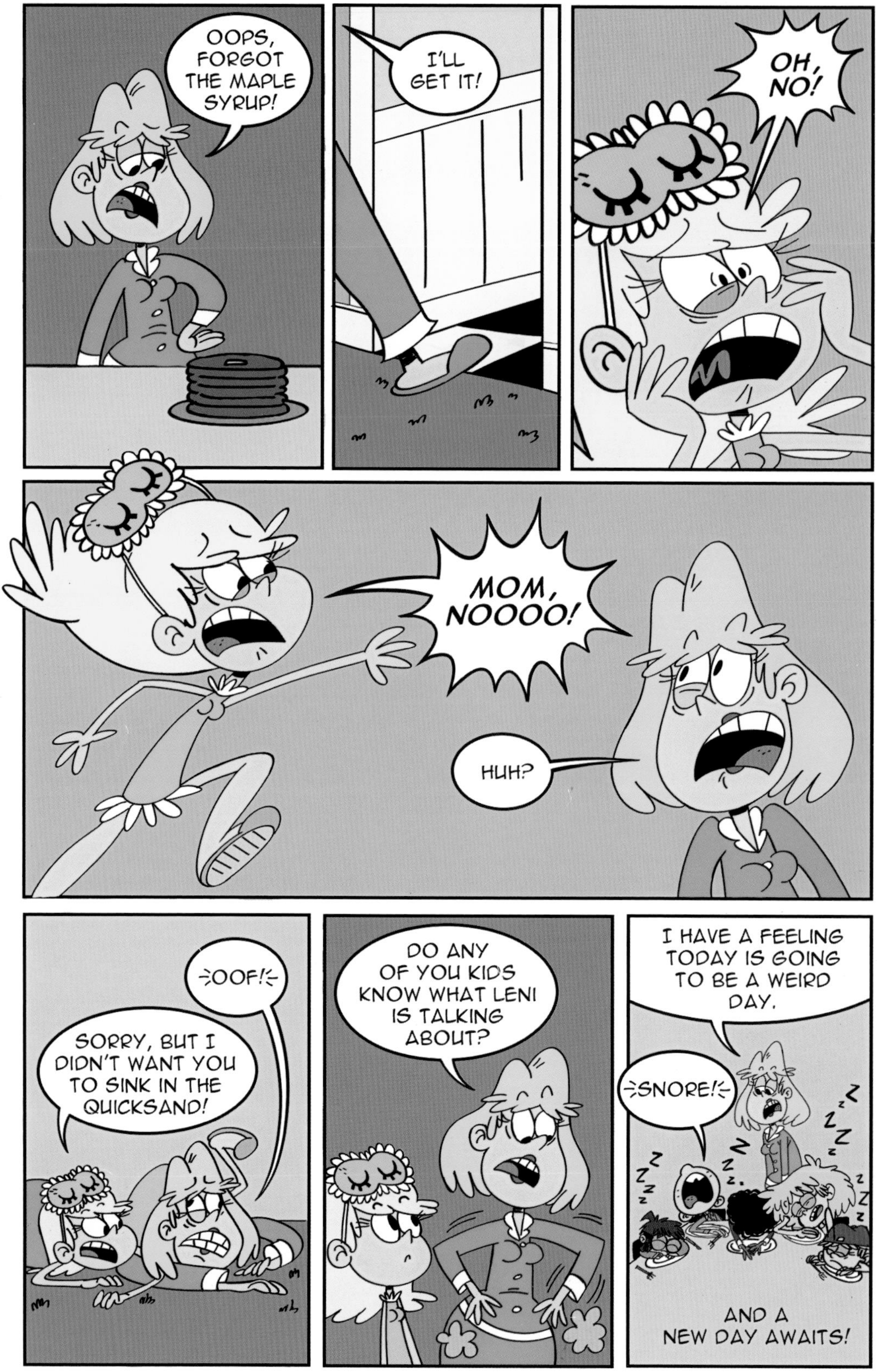
OOPS, FORGOT THE MAPLE SYRUP!
I'LL GET IT!
OH, NO!
MOM, NOOOO!
HUH?
OOF!
SORRY, BUT I DIDN'T WANT YOU TO SINK IN THE QUICKSAND!
DO ANY OF YOU KIDS KNOW WHAT LENI IS TALKING ABOUT?
I HAVE A FEELING TODAY IS GOING TO BE A WEIRD DAY.
SNORE!
Z Z Z
AND A NEW DAY AWAITS!

WATCH OUT FOR PAPERCUTZ

Welcome to the back of the fifth family-filled, fashionable, fast-paced, fabulous THE LOUD HOUSE graphic novel from Papercutz—those felicitous folks dedicated to publishing great graphic novels for all ages. I'm Jim Salicrup, the Editor-in-Chief and Explainer-of-Things, here to explain some things…

Back in THE LOUD HOUSE #3, we mentioned that THE LOUD HOUSE #4, the next graphic novel would be entitled "The Struggle is Real," and as all true THE LOUD HOUSE graphic novel fans already know, THE LOUD HOUSE #4 was actually entitled "Family Tree." So you might be wondering, what happened?

Here's what happened: When we got word that THE LOUD HOUSE ULTIMATE TREEHOUSE app was coming, we just couldn't wait to tell you, but it was still TOP SECRET! Oh, sure we suddenly changed the title, whipped up a new cover featuring a treehouse, and even added an all-new story featuring Lincoln building a treehouse, and added a gazillion tree-references into the Watch Out for Papercutz page, but we never spilled the beans! We promised to reveal what all the tree-talk was about in THE LOUD HOUSE #5, but we did say you'd find out faster on Instagram at @TheLoudHouseCartoon and on Facebook.com/TheLoudHouse, and we're sure you did! If you've been playing THE LOUD HOUSE ULTIMATE TREEHOUSE game, we're also sure you can see why we were so excited.

Meanwhile, we had yet another crazy idea! We usually do short stories for each graphic novel because we've been working with the super-talented writers and artists from THE LOUD HOUSE show itself, and they don't have time to do much more than a short comics story while they're busy working on the animated TV series.

But what if we came up with an overall theme, like the entire graphic novel taking place over the course of a single night in THE LOUD HOUSE? It would still be a bunch of fun short stories, but when presented altogether it could feel like one big story, right? That's how we came up with THE LOUD HOUSE #5 "After Dark," where we've explored all that goes bump in the night (not just Leni sleepwalking) in Lincoln's home. We hope you enjoyed it. Now, what crazy ideas will we come up with for LOUD HOUSE #6? There's only one way to find out, and that's to be sure to look for THE LOUD HOUSE #6, coming soon!

Thanks!

Jim

STAY IN TOUCH!

EMAIL: salicrup@papercutz.com
WEB: papercutz.com
TWITTER: @papercutzgn
INSTAGRAM: @papercutzgn
FACEBOOK: PAPERCUTZGRAPHICNOVELS
FANMAIL: Papercutz, 160 Broadway, Suite 700, East Wing, New York, NY 10038

See some more ghosts with this excerpt from NICKELODEON PANDEMONIUM! #3!

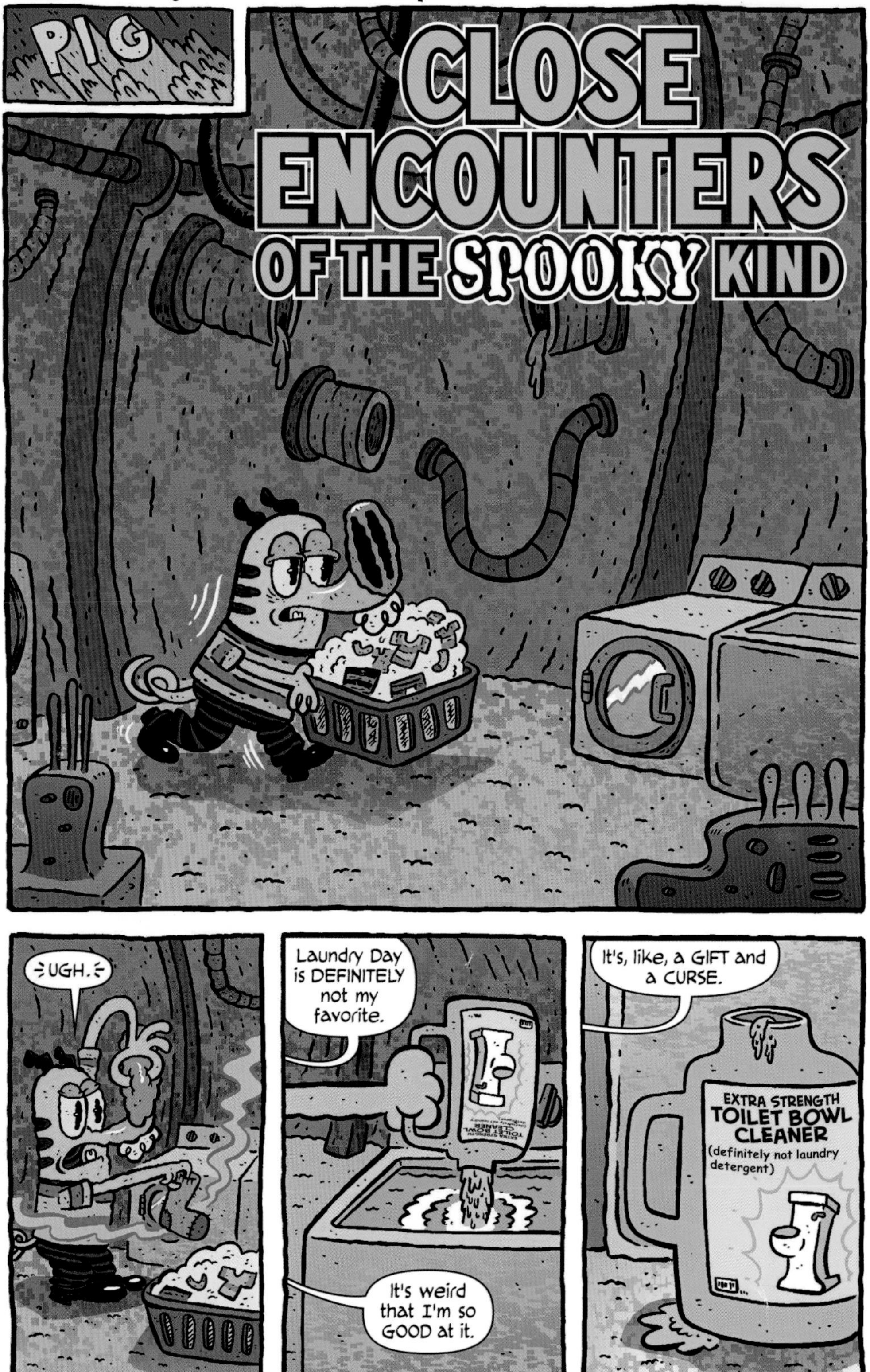
PIG
CLOSE ENCOUNTERS OF THE SPOOKY KIND
UGH.
Laundry Day is DEFINITELY not my favorite.
It's weird that I'm so GOOD at it.
It's, like, a GIFT and a CURSE.
EXTRA STRENGTH TOILET BOWL CLEANER (definitely not laundry detergent)

Eric Esquivel–Writer, David DeGrand–Artist, Laurie E. Smith & Matt Herms–Colorists, Tom Orzechowski–Letterer

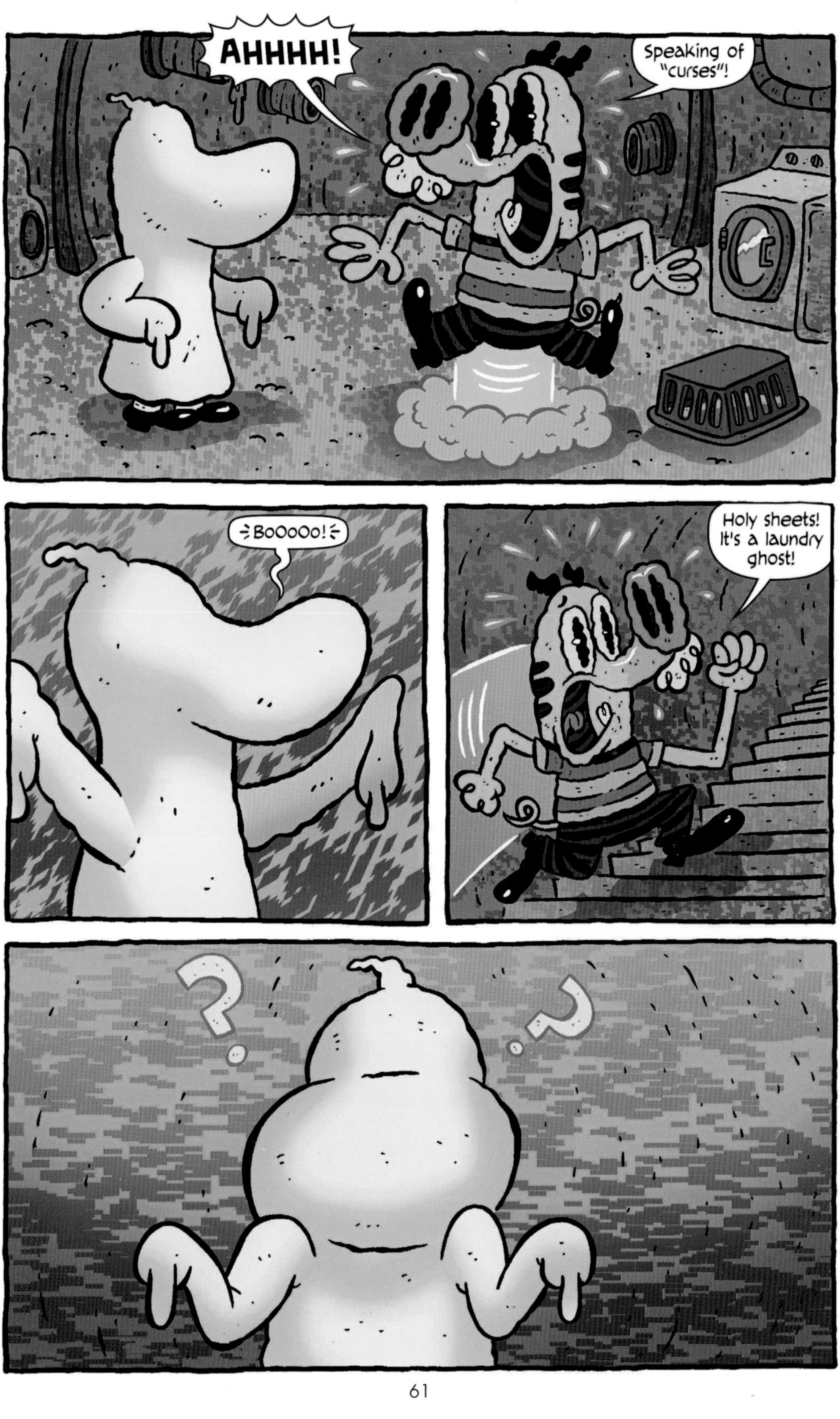
AHHHH!
Speaking of "curses"!
BoOOOo!
Holy sheets! It's a laundry ghost!
?
?

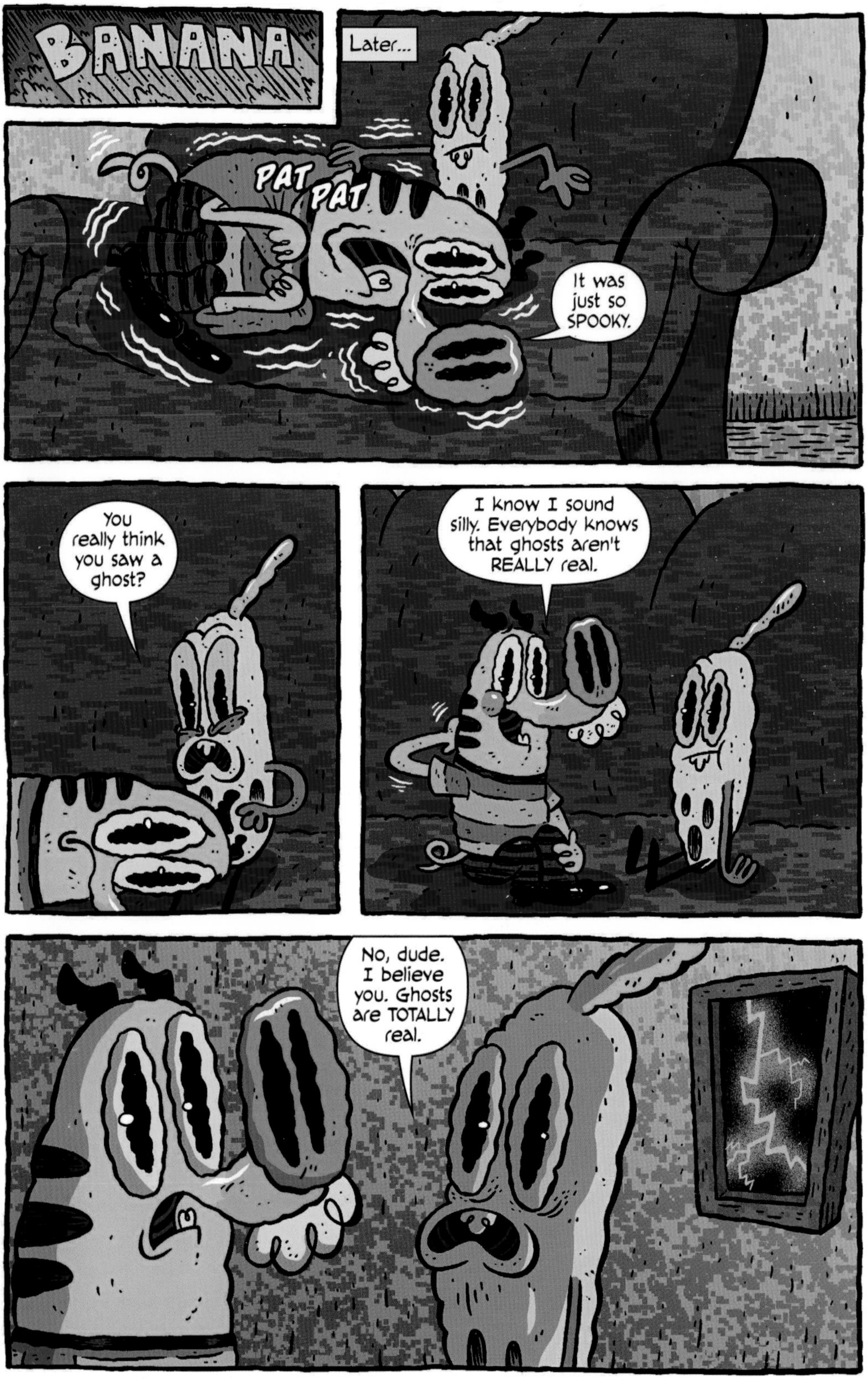
BANANA
Later...
PAT PAT
It was just so SPOOKY.
You really think you saw a ghost?
I know I sound silly. Everybody knows that ghosts aren't REALLY real.
No, dude. I believe you. Ghosts are TOTALLY real.

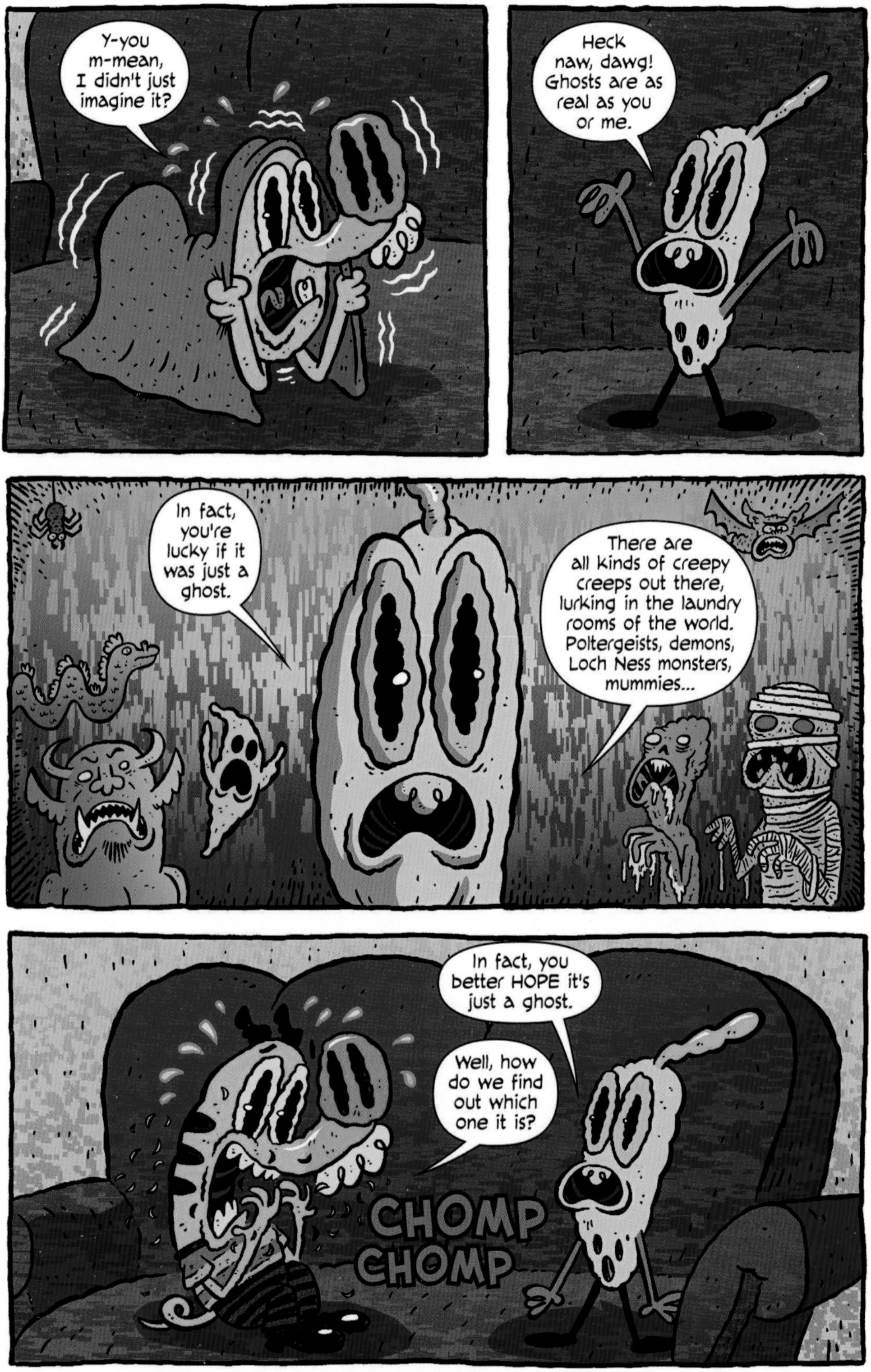
Y-you m-mean, I didn't just imagine it?
Heck naw, dawg! Ghosts are as real as you or me.
In fact, you're lucky if it was just a ghost.
There are all kinds of creepy creeps out there, lurking in the laundry rooms of the world. Poltergeists, demons, Loch Ness monsters, mummies...
In fact, you better HOPE it's just a ghost.
Well, how do we find out which one it is?
CHOMP CHOMP

Pick up NICKELODEON PANDEMONIUM! #3 for the hair-raising conclusion, plus more stories from THE LOUD HOUSE!

LIVE LOUD!

THE LOUD HOUSE
ULTIMATE TREEHOUSE APP

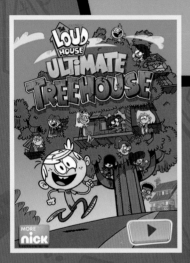

Build the ultimate towering tree house with **Lincoln Loud**!

Free to download on Apple and Android devices.

THE LOUD HOUSE
LISTEN OUT LOUD PODCAST

Get ready to hang with **The Loud House** family like never before!

Listen to new episodes of their podcast, **Listen Out Loud**, on all podcast apps, Nickelodeon's YouTube channel or the Nick App!

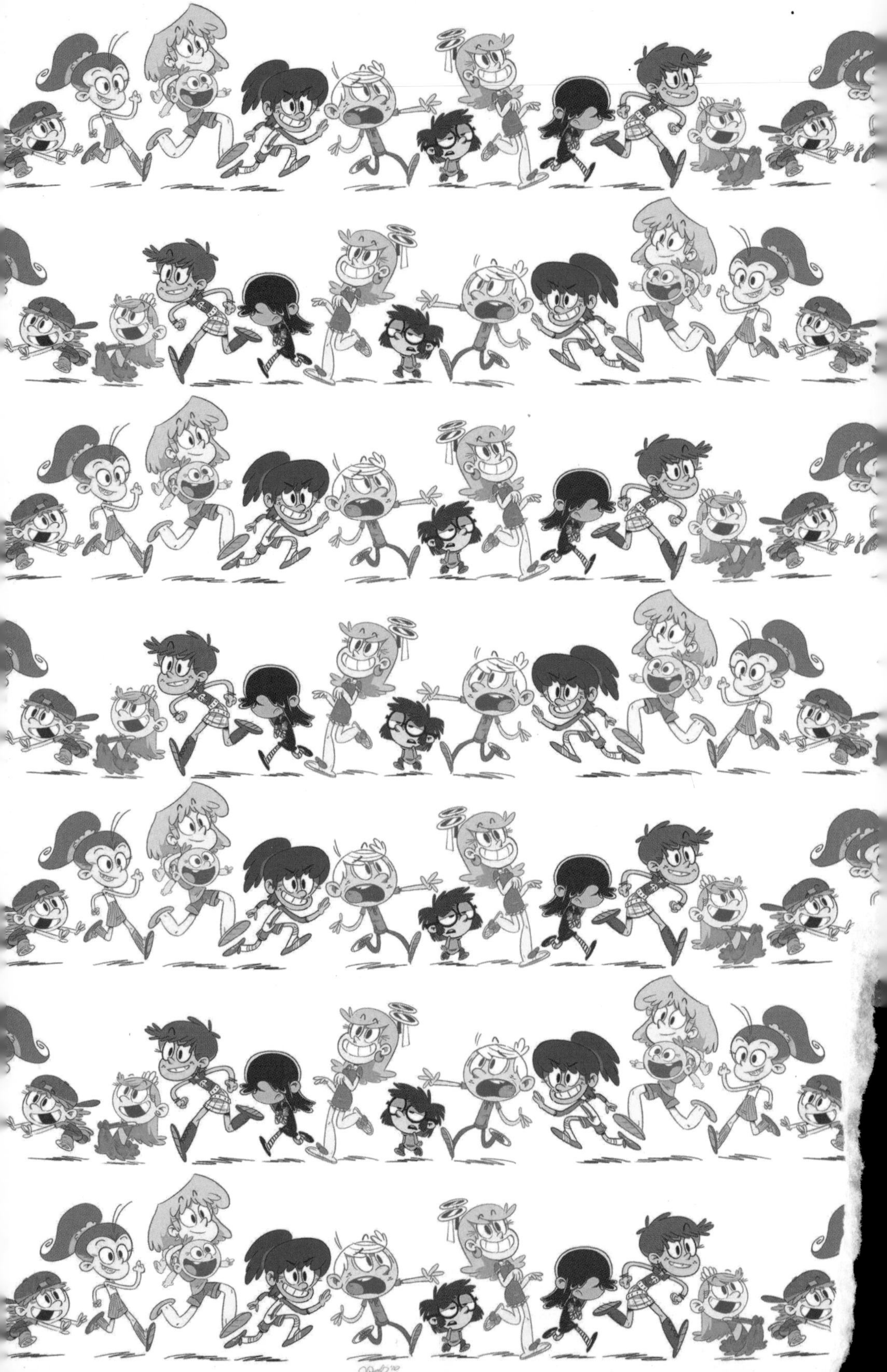